KILLER, RIDE HOME

Also by this author available from New English Library:

FLASHFLOOD

Killer, Ride Home

GIL MARTIN

NEW ENGLISH LIBRARY
TIMES MIRROR

A New English Library Original Publication, 1978

*

FIRST NEL PAPERBACK EDITION FEBRUARY 1978

*

NEL Books are published by New English Library Limited from Barnard's Inn, Holborn, London EC1N 2JR
Made and printed in Great Britain by Cox & Wyman Ltd, London, Reading and Fakenham

45003184 5

CHAPTER ONE

HARVEY called me out because he knew I had sold my gun. He wouldn't have had the guts to do it, otherwise. Even so, I was sure he wouldn't go through with it; it takes more than courage to shoot a man down in cold blood, I should know. It takes a mind that is dead to emotion, or numbed with despair.

So I kept walking, holding those two fistfuls of money, heading for the door, with my back to him. In spite of knowing him and his cowardice I couldn't help feeling the cold prickle of my hair crawling on my scalp as I realised he had pulled out that prissy-looking lethal little Derringer and had it pointed at my back.

He howled again, 'Get back to this here table you lousy two-bit amateur! I ain't finished yet—'

I kept moving and reached the door and he still hadn't pulled the trigger, so I guessed I had been right. He wasn't going to. 'I have, Harvey. You're cleaned out.' I turned in the doorway and faced him. He stood puffing and red-faced, sweating a little with that gun wavering in his shaky hand.

'Goddam your eyes! Never were nothing but a corny-assed country boy. You'll never get another game here,' he yelled.

I grinned and raised my hands clenched around the money. 'This'll see me through.' Harvey's mouth opened and shut in speechless frustration and I went through the door and stepped on to the boardwalk, breathing in the cold San Francisco night air with a kind of relief, feeling the tension go out of me now that I had crawled out of another tight spot with my skin still in one piece. I wondered how much longer that kind of luck would hold for me.

It was late and the place was alive with shadowy figures going about their business. I wasn't the kind of man who would attract attention or give reason to believe I was worth robbing, I knew that, but all the same I ducked into the nearest dark alleyway and crammed those dollar bills into my vest and shirt pockets then buttoned my shabby coat, just in case.

Harvey wasn't too trustworthy either. It was just possible he would send someone after me, so it was necessary for me to get back to my room without waiting around for anything to happen. As it was, I passed an alley where two Chinese boys were going through the pockets of a drunken sailor who lay half in, half out of the black mouth of the passageway. They looked up at me as I passed, but I turned my head away and that satisfied them. Anyways they didn't come after me.

I came to a better lit part of town, and the street lamps cast golden pools in the rain-wet streets. The reek of the harbour was never so strong at night as it was in the heat of the day, and above the darkened buildings I could see the masts of some foreign schooner outlined against the starry sky. There was a fight on the next corner, in the shadows, where dark figures weaved backwards and forwards. I could hear grunts and gasps of pain as knife blades flashed and I stepped around them. One of the figures reeled backwards into me and I heaved him away, pushing him back into the fray and walked on, feeling Harvey's money weighing heavy in my pockets.

I got back safely, resisting the temptation to visit one of the saloons on my way. The ache for a drink was becoming a pain in my gut, raw and rasping, but for once there was something else to do with my money, someplace else to go, a plan to be made that was even more important than drinking myself into that blessed oblivion I needed so badly.

In that one squalid room that sometimes I paid for and sometimes I didn't, I bolted the door and drew the tattered, moth-eaten drapes before I lit the lamp, then I sat on the rumpled bed and drew out Harvey's money, spread it on the stained sheets and counted it. 2,500 dollars, by God! Harvey wouldn't forget that in a hurry. The quicker I got out of here and armed myself, the better I'd feel. The thought of all that money in my pockets as I walked through San Francisco's crazy night-time streets made me sweat with delayed reaction.

2,500 dollars, more than enough to get me where I wanted to go and show Abe that my life wasn't all lows. I guess there hadn't been too many high spots, whisky and women and defending myself had seen to that, but this time I had a reason to go home and I swore to myself that I would show him. 'This time, Abe,' I said out loud.

When I had taken out the money I had won from Harvey, I'd taken out Aunt Tilda's letter, too. It lay screwed up on the bed, among the dollar bills, so I picked it up, straightened it and re-read it.

> 'My dear adopted son, Saul, [It said,] it's many months since I wrote you, and not having heard for must be two years, not a word 'cept bad ones, I feel I must write again and pray this ignorant old black woman's letter will reach you. I'm getting very old now and well-nigh bed-ridden, but your pa was always good to me, if blind to you, and he 'lows me to stay on in my house with blood-son Jed to watch over me and gran'daughter Salena who's growin' fast. You know how her ma, Jubilee, run off.
>
> Things is much the same at the ranch. It's goin' real good and all the horses get bigger and finer, and the mares are breedin' real well. Knowin' you don't have much interest with the way things are here, I won't say too much, but I feel you ought to know your Pa's married again to a migrant woman of German stock. She's a real nice lady, and very pleasant to all of us.
>
> I'm sendin' this letter care of Jed who's goin' to Californy to visit his wife's folks. Last I heard you was headin' that way, so Jed's kin will pass it around until it gets to you.
>
> I would like to see you afore I die, but I don't hold much hope for it. You was always a good boy to me, no matter what they say about you. Your lovin' Aunt Tilda.

The words blurred in front of my eyes as I looked at her wavering old-woman's scrawl and I felt the warmth of her affection flood through me, even across all those miles of desert and prairie and mountain. She had done her best for me, and it still wasn't enough. It could never be.

I lay back on the unmade bed and rolled a smoke and

thought about her and Abe and Abe's new wife, goddam her eyes. Tomorrow, I'd leave and when I reached home I'd see what it was that made Abe think someone else could ever replace my mother. If this German thought she would have things her own way, I'd show her how wrong she could be. I wondered if she even knew I existed. But, behind it all was the deeper need; the always hidden almost subconscious longing for something that I could never have, because of what I was. The only reason I ever went home and always left again. Because, once more, I'd failed. Things never changed. This time maybe, I thought, then pushed the thought away.

Early the next morning, I gathered my few belongings and rolled them in my saddle blanket. It was all I had left of the time I had owned a horse. Pushing the money into my pockets, I left the room in that tumbledown boarding-house and walked out of there. I was nervous at first, thinking Harvey and his men would be around, but I didn't see anyone so I hurried over to the horse trader's place before they got around to making any plans for getting Harvey's money back to him. Even though I had won it fair, I knew it wouldn't sit easy with him and he wouldn't take his loss for too long.

There wasn't much in the way of good horseflesh here, and the trader must have seen me around. He wasn't interested and I guess I looked like a bum, but he began to perk up when I showed him a fistful of dollars. I said, 'You don't want my money, I'll take it someplace else. Can't you do any better than that?' I indicated the herd of broken-down, hard-ridden broncos in the pen.

'Now there is one in the corral out back,' he said, his eyes bright on the money in my fist, 'but he'll cost you a hundred. He's good. I was going to keep him myself.'

'Show him to me. I'll tell you if he's worth a hundred.'

The trader shrugged. 'I'm letting him go cheap at that. He was left here to pay a debt. I guess I could get more.'

I snapped impatiently, 'I haven't got all day.'

We went and looked through the slats of the corral fence at a big black gelding, near sixteen hands high with good long racehorse legs and a head set high and proud. He had big, intelligent eyes and a strong, smooth movement. I said, 'No arguing. I'm offering a hundred, take it or leave it. If I wasn't in such a hurry, I'd be doing the arguing.'

He took the money and decided not to bargain over the saddle, bridle and saddle-bags I bought next. It took a while for me to catch the gelding and saddle him. I guess he hadn't been ridden for a while because he was spooky and vicious, cow-kicking when I cinched him and taking a lunge for me with his long yellow teeth. The trader stood by, counting his money and grinning when the gelding bucked as I mounted. But it was good to be in the saddle again, after all this time, and I guessed the horse would cool off with the miles we had to cover. Besides, I liked an animal with spirit, and I had the feeling that I would need it before long. The day was passing swiftly and Harvey's temper was probably reaching boiling point.

The gelding shot out of the corral as though he had a burr up his tail and we were half-way along the street before I could haul him in. He danced and sweated all the way to the nearest general store where I tied him firmly to the hitch rail. The store keeper must have seen me around too because he wasn't too friendly and examined the pile of purchases I made with doubt and suspicion on his mean-eyed face. I enjoyed not showing him the money till the last minute, and watched the change in his attitude with a wry inward smile.

He even helped me choose my new clothes and packed the old ones in one of my new saddle-bags. My last buy was a good second-hand Colt .45, something like the one I had had to sell to keep me in the liquor that kept me sane. The gun would have to keep me alive on the way home. Booze could wait awhile, even if it was going to well-nigh finish me, I'd gone without it before and I could do it again, I thought as I filled my new gun belt and loaded the Colt. Carrying my provisions, I went outside again where the gelding was stamping impatiently, sweating a little already. I said to him, 'Calm down, feller, you'll be moving soon. More than you want to,' and slapped his neck before fixing the laden bags behind the saddle.

It wasn't hard leaving San Francisco. It had never been hard leaving anywhere, with no one to say goodbye to and nothing but bad times and sorry memories attached to each place. I did stop for a while, on a hill, looking down on the spread-out scene of the harbour and the city and the blue sea, sparkling with sunshine, stretching way out to the horizon. Dark shapes of ships and boats rode silently at anchor in the bay, and above me, even this far inland, seagulls circled and called. It took only a moment for me to look and store away the memory, and then I turned that skittish gelding and rode down the hill into the wild country, leaving San Francisco to drop out of sight as though it had never existed.

I followed the road for a while, leaving tracks on the side in the mud from last night's rain then, for some reason, I began to feel jumpy and took off at an angle, forcing the gelding into a lope, away from the trail but still following it at a distance. There was some instinct in me that warned me I wasn't clear yet. As I rode, I put my hand down to feel the security of the Colt and slide it a little from the holster, just to make sure it was still there.

It was well into the day when I reached a stream and stopped to allow the gelding to drink. I dismounted, loosened the girth and let him suck up the water, while I rolled a smoke and sat by him thinking of the peace and quietness of the countryside and how good it was to be moving on at last. A lark was filling the sky with his song and the sound was liquid and sweet compared with the harsh cry of the gulls that had filled my head for too long. His song stopped suddenly and I saw the small brown bird plummet to earth and watched him as he ran after he alighted. In that stillness after the music, the shot was twice as startling.

A bullet buzzed past me and I heard it strike the surface of the water and skip, ricocheting somewhere on the far stream bank. The gelding leaped and snorted and I dropped my cigarette and raced for the reins before he should leave me. I swore at the same time. That goddam Harvey, I'd almost forgotten him. Another sharp crack, and a second bullet came uncomfortably close as I fumbled at the cinch. I glanced behind me quickly and saw them coming, there were three of them but still a ways off.

I was glad I hadn't pushed that horse. He was still fresh and ready to go. Together we splashed through the stream and up the muddy bank on the other side. I heard the suck of the gelding's hooves as he struggled up then hit hard ground at a gallop. Snatching another look behind me I saw the three gunnies spread out and spur their horses on. I thought grimly, if Harvey wants it all back he's out of luck, I spent some, and urged the horse faster. I could hear the air puffing in his lungs and was glad I had chosen him for his speed.

The country was too open for a while. My only hope right then was to outrun them, but they were still on my tail and I knew I wouldn't lose them. They had stopped shooting, at that range and speed they would be wasting bullets, but I wasn't fooled into thinking they weren't going to try again as soon as they got the chance. Now that they had spooked me, they thought I was on the run for good but I had other plans. All I needed was the right place.

As the gelding puffed under me and I crouched low over his neck, I kept my eyes darting, looking for my chance. The horse was almost played out and I was beginning to feel the cold clutch of despair when I found the place. We had come down a draw and for a moment my pursuers were out of sight, still coming up the other side of the rise. To my left was a dip and a dried-up gully that could have been hollowed by some long-gone flashflood. I wrenched the gelding around, almost throwing him off balance, and headed for the dip. We hit it throwing dust and I hauled in the horse and leaped from the saddle, drawing my gun at the same time. I pushed the gelding along the gully and hoped to God nothing showed. I guessed it didn't. He was so tired he stood shaking and sweating, with his head almost touching the ground. I threw myself forward, looking over the edge of the natural rampart just as those three followers breasted the rise and reined in, silhouetted against the bright noon sky.

I cursed under my breath because they were still well apart. I'd have to pick them off one at a time, odds I didn't like.

They paused, puzzled. I should have been in plain view, to their minds, heading off into the distance. Now, I had disappeared. I could almost read what they were thinking. From where they were, the gully would be no more than a shadow on the plain. I hadn't seen it until I was almost on it. It was certain they would have to come down the rise if they were going to find me at all. They were well out of range of my handgun, but it didn't worry me too much, they only had pistols, too. At least we were even on that score.

I waited while they watched, then one of them turned his horse towards the others and they conferred a moment, sitting there on the skyline. A fly buzzed irritatingly around my eyes and I brushed at it, wiping sweat from my forehead and blinking to keep those damned bushwhackers in focus. 'Come on,' I said between my teeth, 'make up your minds.'

They decided then. Two of them rode on, coming down the draw towards me, leaving the third still sitting his horse on the rise, covering them. I felt my bowels clench as they came nearer. It was only a matter of time. I felt sure I'd get two, but it was number three who fazed me. Damn it, it was my money, I won it fair.

The two came nearer, eyes searching the ground, picking up a hoof-print here and there. They still hadn't stumbled across my gully. I stretched out my gun hand and thumbed back the hammer, glad of the six full chambers, sure I'd need them. They were almost in range when they stopped and waved at the gunny on the hill, pointing forward and down, showing him they were still on my trail. I watched him start forward and come on down at a trot to join them. Now they were all three together and their guns were holstered. I felt my mouth curl upward in tight anticipation and a kind of elation at their stupidity. Where in hell did they think I was?

Slowly they came forward, bunched, and rode into range. Now I had them. As usual, when I used a gun, I was filled with that momentary, heart-stopping memory that clutched my brain and twisted my belly. The sickness rose up in my throat and I sobbed as I pulled the trigger, once, the chamber revolved, I pulled back the hammer, twice, again the mechanism and one more touch of the trigger. It was done! I sank down, my face on my outstretched arm.

When I raised my head at last I saw a horse standing, bemused, over the prone figure of its rider, its reins trailing in the dirt. Far away another horse was galloping wildly, its saddle empty and its rider, one foot still in the stirrup, jouncing and dragging behind it, arms flying bonelessly in the cloud of dust that surrounded them both. The third horse stood nearer, its head drooping. Across the saddle, the gunny lay forward, his face hidden in the animal's mane, his arms hanging limply each side of its withers.

I came to my feet cautiously, ready for any sudden move from the wounded men. There was none. Just the same I had the gun ready—there were still three bullets to use and I would shoot again if I had to. I stepped out of the gully and made my way over to them. The nearest horse's rider was still alive, but only just. He wouldn't make it till sundown, shot through the chest and one lung gone, the blood that seeped out filled with air bubbles. I took the horse by the reins and led it over to the still figure on the ground. He was quite dead, shot neatly through the head, where I had aimed to put the bullet. I was sorry about the man still lying over his horse, I had meant him to be dead, quick and neat, no suffering, like his companion.

I turned to the rider of the horse I held. Blood was coming out of him and running down the horse's flanks. His head was turned towards me and though his eyes were glazed he still had some consciousness. I said to him, 'Harvey send you?'

There was no answer and I guess I didn't expect one. I turned his horse. 'I'm sending you back. If you live to see him, tell him I said thanks for the money. I got things to do with it that he's got no share in. I don't aim to see him again.'

There was a saddle rope attached to the horn, so I took it down and passed it around him a couple of times, fixing him in the saddle then I took off my hat and brought it down across the horse's rump. I yelled 'Hah!' and it leaped forward and raced away, back the way it had come, its rider's head bouncing up and down on its neck with the movement.

I took one more look at the dead man on the ground, then caught his horse and unsaddled and unbridled it. I turned it around and sent it on its way, too. It stood a better chance of survival in this country unhampered by harness. As for the last man, the one who was probably still being dragged somewhere over into the next county, I couldn't do anything about him, I guess.

CHAPTER TWO

AFTER that episode, for more than one reason, I knew I'd have to keep to the wilderness route. I don't think Harvey would have sent any more gunnies after me, but I had a lot of money and in spite of caution, it can show, I don't know how. I couldn't afford to let anyone suspect I might be worth picking over. It wasn't only the money kept me away from people and towns and railroad tracks. Where there is habitation there are saloons and I couldn't let even a smell of liquor come near me. To put it baldly, I didn't trust myself, so I kept out of temptation's path and did it the hard way.

We made the whole journey on foot, that gelding and I, and it took weeks. Sometimes, I'll confess, the loneliness and the need for a drink became a harsh craving that made me roll around with stomach cramps and my temper was so short I wouldn't have blamed that big horse if he had taken the first opportunity to get shot of me. I guess horses aren't like that. They put up with uppity owners and make allowances for shortcomings that no human would tolerate. Sometimes, I had to suck pebbles to ease the liquor hunger and rolled too many smokes and made vile-tasting coffee more often than I needed to, but I stayed sober all the way.

I had shucked my fine duds and put on my old clothes and let my beard grow and must have looked as bad as I felt. There'd be time to freshen up before I reached the ranch.

One morning I crossed a county line and knew home was only half a day's ride away. I altered my angle of approach deliberately so that I wouldn't have to pass through town. It was years since I had set foot there, and I felt I needed a little more time before I faced the townsfolk. I guess it was cowardice. Already I was feeling the tremors that always passed through me when I reached Abe's place and the thought of that confrontation had me as shaky and weak as though I were still the child I had been. No amount of dollar bills, no fine clothes, no blood horse could ever make me feel fit to stand up to him and command his respect, even now. Whatever strong urges I had had, curiosity or even need, were washed away as I neared the spread.

Nervous as a kitten, I stopped by a water hole, washed up and even tried to shave off my beard. Then I dressed in those new clothes again, and the last thing I did was to unbuckle that gun belt and push the Colt and the ammunition right down to the bottom of the saddle-bag. They would stay there, I thought, until it was time for me to leave again. Suddenly, they felt unwholesome and soiled and for a moment I was tempted to take them out again and drown the lot in the pool, but I overrode that thought. I never knew when I would need them and I had been too long unarmed. So I remounted, set my face towards the ranch and rode on.

It was there at last. On a rise I pulled in and looked down at Abe's spread, my fingers white on the reins, my jaw clenched so tight my teeth ached and my heart beating fast with apprehension. The place looked bigger, more spacious with new fenced corrals and the specks of horses grazing in them. On all sides the tree-dotted pastures lay peacefully in the sun and I could see more stock than I had ever remembered there. Abe's place looked prosperous. Nothing had changed at the Big House, even if he had taken another wife. At least, it seemed the same from the outside, long and low and sprawling whitely with its covered porches and splashes of flower borders. Away to one side, I could see the workers' shacks, neat and square with tiny vegetable gardens. Abe had had a couple of new ones built, I noticed, and there under the big old apple tree was Aunt Tilda's shack, small and homely, just the way I remembered it. At last my heels told the gelding to go on and he moved along the path, head up, interested in this new place, a little too quickly for my liking, but I let him go.

As I took the main trail and rode under the gate with the name 'Bowen' arched overhead, I looked around for a familiar face. There were a few men around, mostly coloured hands and some I knew but whose names I had forgotten. They looked across at me with seeming unconcern, and one or two frowned in concentration then recognition, and most showed curiosity. Those I didn't know had surely heard of me because, from some of the covert glances they sent at me and then each other, I think they expected me to have cloven hoofs and horns.

I hoped I wouldn't have to go looking for Jed, but I had hardly turned the gelding's head for Tilda's house when a tall, lean figure detached itself from a group by one of the corrals and came striding towards me, his teeth a slash of white in his handsome black face.

'Saul,' he called, 'Saul, boy, it's good to see you!'

As usual, his welcome warmed me and made me feel it was all worthwhile if I only came back to him and Tilda. I dismounted and waited for him to reach me, grinning like a fool myself. 'Jed,' I said and held out my hand. He pumped it vigorously for a long time, one hand on my shoulder. 'Boy, you're lookin' good, real good.' His eyes took me in and the travel stained gelding. He nodded at it. 'Fine horse. You been doin' well.'

'Not bad.' I felt a twinge of guilt at his surprised relief. 'You're looking great yourself. Little older is all.'

'We all get that way.' He laughed delightedly, 'Ma will be fit to be tied when she sees you. I think she'd given up hope.'

'I'm sorry. I came as soon as I got the letter, but you know how it is. It was months old when it reached me.'

'Yeah, I know how it is. I'm glad you got it anyways.' He looked me over again. 'You come from Californy?'

'All the way.'

'That's a fur piece. I guess you'll be hungry. There's some fried chicken left up at Ma's. You're welcome to it.' He hesitated and glanced at me swiftly, ' 'Less you want to go to the Big House.'

'I'd be obliged, Jed. There's nothing at the Big House to interest me,' I lied.

'You feel the same way?' I had turned and Jed fell into step beside me, heading for Tilda's shack.

'Nothing's changed.'

Jed cleared his throat, 'Something has.'

'You mean Abe marrying again?'

'Ma mention it in her letter?' There was relief in Jed's voice at not having to explain.

'I came to see Tilda. She said she was sick.'

Jed shook his head, 'She hasn't got long.' We were silent a while as we walked. 'You remember my girl, Salena?' Jed said suddenly.

'Skinny kid with pigtails.'

He laughed, 'Well, she's growed a bit. She's fifteen now. She tends to Ma and does the cookin'. Works up at the Big House too. She's better than an adult woman. I'm proud of her.'

We reached the front door and Jed took the gelding from me and hitched it to a low hanging bough of the apple tree. It started in to helping itself to the fruit. 'Hey, Ma!' Jed ran up the steps and opened the front door. 'I got a surprise for you. A real good one!'

I followed him when he beckoned me in, into the neat spotless room I remembered so well and across the polished floor to Tilda's room. The door was open and she was lying in the bed, propped up on pillows. From where I was I could hear the breath rasping in her throat. It hurt to see how wasted and frail she was, but her eyes, when she turned her head, were bright and alive with pleasure and excitement as she saw me.

'Saul,' her voice quavered, 'my boy Saul. He's come home.' She held out her black, thin arms and the skin was wrinkled, hanging loose. I went past Jed and sat on the edge of the bed, cradling her tiny form in my arms and rested my cheek on the wiry, white hair. She meant a lot to me, my adopted Ma.

I drew away and took her face in my hands, looking down into her bright black eyes. 'On a day like this,' I said, 'you should be up doing your chores. Why, you're lying abed like a queen.'

She laughed a little and began to cough and I was alarmed at the violence of the spasm. She stopped at last and gasped, 'You see, boy? You see? I'm just a useless old woman now.' She shook her head then took my hands in hers and held them against her cheeks. 'But it does me good to see you and you look so fine and handsome, I'm better already.' She frowned at me playfully, 'Your hair needs cutting,' and she stroked it where it lay long at the back of my neck.

I said meekly, 'Yes, Ma'am,' and behind me Jed laughed.

He said, 'I'll fetch Salena and we'll fix Saul some vittles. You talk to him, Ma.' He went away.

'Are you staying, boy? Just a while?' Tilda's blackberry eyes became swimming and anxious.

'Now I've seen you, Aunt Tilda, I ain't fixin' to be anywhere but here for a while.'

She smiled, 'Now I can set back and die happy. I've been hangin' on just waitin' for you.'

I feigned alarm, 'I ain't figurin' on stayin' another hundred years.'

She laughed again and had another paroxysm of coughing. I hated to see her that way. Childishly, I wanted her to be the same as when I had last seen her. I waited till she had settled back against her pillows then asked, 'How's Abe?'

A shadow passed her eyes, 'You haven't seen him?'

'He doesn't know I'm here. I guess it wouldn't make any difference.'

'I wish you could be friends. It's been so hard on you.'

'It's too late. We're both set in our ways. Can't change now.'

She said, 'You get my letter? About him marryin' again?'

I nodded, 'It was a surprise.'

'For all of us. But she's a real nice lady.'

I shrugged.

'She knows about you,' Tilda said. 'I mean she knows Abe has a son. She once asked Jed if you ever visited the spread.'

I smiled wryly, 'I wonder how much she knows.'

'If Abe told her, she don't know the full truth of it, or what a good boy you really are.'

'Who cares?' Tilda's trust hurt me too.

She reached up and touched my hair. 'I do, boy, I do. It grieves me.' We were silent for a moment then she said, 'Tell me about Californy and all you been doin'.'

So I told her about my travels, touching on the places I had been, the sights I had seen, but there was no way I would tell her what I had been doing. She held my hand and her eyes grew bigger with awe. 'I can see it like I had been there,' she said at last. 'You always was a good talker. I can smell the sea and hear the sea birds. I never seen the sea,' she finished wistfully.

Jed called me then and I left her, smiling, at peace. He took me into the kitchen where a trim black girl stood at the sink, putting food on a plate. She turned and she was mighty pretty with a straight thin nose and long-lashed dark eyes and the blooming body of near maturity. She smiled at me shyly.

'This here's Salena,' Jed said, 'You remember?'

'You didn't look like that when I left, Salena,' I grinned, 'You're real good-lookin'.'

She lowered her eyes in embarrassment, 'I remember you, Mister Saul. I still got the wooden doll you carved for me.'

She came to the table and put the plate on it. 'You like to eat now?' Her eyes met mine again and there was something in them, a kind of knowing woman's look, unfulfilled yet promising. She was too young for what feelings went through me and certainly too old for a wooden doll.

I sat down and began to eat and Jed sat opposite me. Salena busied herself at the sink. Jed said, 'I should be workin' I guess, but I got a good excuse.'

I said, 'I'll come with you, when you go, and have myself a look around. Abe's made some changes.'

'A few,' Jed nodded, 'All good.' He was silent a moment. 'You tell Ma much?'

I looked up, 'About what?'

'What you been doin'?'

He knew, there was no sense in lying to him. I glanced sideways at Salena. 'I told her where I've been.'

Jed nodded, 'I ain't sayin' there's truth in what I heard, but I never told Ma nothing.'

I said softly, 'Maybe more truth than lies, Jed.'

His eyes met mine levelly. 'You're a man full grown. You

do what you like. 'Tain't none of my business. You look good on it anyways.'

'The devil takes care of his own.' I spoke lightly but it went deeper than I thought it could. I was home, now, among good people and I hoped that none of the evil that clung to me would brush off on them.

Later, I went with Jed and spent the afternoon in the fields watching him and the crew working, remembering how it felt to be involved in hard manual work for the sake of pride in a job well done, and recalling the good, clean sense of it. For a while the others watched me warily, then relaxed when they saw I was human and probably harmless. I didn't know I would care, but I did and it hurt a little.

It was almost dark when they finished and Jed and I walked away through the gathering shadows towards the silent grove of trees where the marble of my mother's grave shone palely between the looming shrubs. I glanced at it out of the corners of my eyes and felt again the familiar tremor which I had never outgrown. One day, I had always feared, I would pass by and she would be there, staring at me with eyes full of reproach, pale and ghastly and inexorable. There was nothing but the marble headstone in that grove now, and fresh flowers glowing in a vase set into the stone edging. I made up my mind that I would go there alone soon and force myself to face the memories and terrible guilt.

Our way lay through the yard in front of the Big House, and as we approached it I saw the lamps were lit in the living-room that I had not entered for twenty years. I turned my head to look at it as we drew abreast of it and I could sense Jed's curiosity about my reaction. As though it were planned, the door opened and a shaft of yellow lamplight fell on the porch throwing my father's shadow, long, almost to my feet. He stood framed in the doorway, his face indiscernible in darkness. I stopped, the old tension rising in me and filling my throat. I was still scared of him. Jed hesitated then walked on, minding his own business.

'Saul.' My father nodded, his voice gruff and hard, the same as usual.

'Abe.' My answer was steady, belying the fear that pulsed senselessly through me.

'You staying long?' He wasn't interested. He had to know.

'I got no plans, yet.'

He nodded again and looked at me for a moment longer then went in and shut the door. I went on slowly to Tilda's cottage and Jed was waiting for me outside.

'How was it?'

I shrugged, 'The same.'

We didn't mention it again that evening. Salena had cooked a good meal and I watched her tend Tilda in a professional way beyond her years. I said, when she was out of the room, 'You've got a good girl there, Jed.'

'I know it, I'm lucky.'

'Good-looking, too.'

'She don't know it.' Jed looked at me thoughtfully, 'It comes natural to her to move and use her eyes that way. She's got feelin's but don't understand them yet. That worries me sometimes. A girl needs her Ma when she gets to that age.'

'I'm sorry about Jubilee running off like that.' Jed's wife hadn't been around long enough for me to make any decisions about her. She had been there before I left, when Salena was little, and once or twice on my previous visits, then she was no longer a part of the family.

'She was bored,' Jed shrugged, 'She was allus a city woman. But it makes Salena twice as precious to me.'

We went out on the porch to smoke, whiling away the evening hours, watching the stars march by over the dark, pleasant pastures, catching the sweet scent of lush grass and horses in the late air. A neighbour from one of the shacks came to talk awhile and we relaxed, the two black men and I, and I was drawn to gratitude at the way they accepted my difference from them, and made allowances for it and showed no tension at my presence.

Tilda and Salena were asleep in Tilda's room when we went in and I found myself lying in the bed that had been mine for so many years, staring up at the familiar ceiling, remembering and not wanting to. I guess it was the confrontation with Abe, and seeing my mother's resting-place again that brought on the nightmares. They had always plagued me, but they seemed worse tonight. It was harder to wake from them, and when I did, the bed was a shambles from my tossing and turning and my throat was dry and parched. The need for a drink was a physical pain. Always, after my dreams I had sought oblivion in a bottle, but there was nothing here to help me. I rose and went to the window and drew in long gulps of fresh air and listened to the night insects chirruping outside. God, I ached for a drink.

I couldn't stand it any longer. I pulled on my pants and went barefoot into the living-room. I lit the lamp and began to search quietly along the shelves, in a dresser, opening and closing doors as silently as I could. There were no bottles, no hint of a drink. My temper rose steadily with my frustration and I picked up the lamp and took it with me into the kitchen, and set it down on the table. I began to search among the jars of preserves and pickles on a shelf. They clinked together, sounding loud in the sleeping silence and, again, there was nothing there. I bent to a small fly-wired container and found a piece of ham and some beef but nothing to drink.

'You-all hungry again, Mister Saul?'

I whirled and the flush burned up my face as I saw Salena standing in the doorway. Her dark eyes were wide with surprise and her pretty teeth were very white as she smiled a little uncertainly. She was wearing a kind of white nightshirt that tied at the neck with ribbons and it reached only to her knees. The sleeves ended at her elbows. I guess she had grown out of it a long time ago, for I could see the youthful swell of her body against the thin fabric and could see the small points of her breasts showing plain.

I swallowed. 'It ain't that, Salena. It's—it's this pain I have. Do you know if your Pa keeps anything to drink? Whisky, something just for medicine?'

She frowned, 'Lawdy, no. I don't think I ever seen him drink, Mister Saul. I'll come he'p you look.'

She came into the room and I could see the long sweep of her slim thighs as she moved. I swallowed and turned away and gripped the edge of the table with my hands so that my knuckles showed white.

When I looked back at her, I saw she had reached up to the shelves I had just searched and I should have told her I knew there was nothing on them, but I was fascinated by her movements and I just stood there watching the hem of her nightshirt ride higher, hating myself.

'Salena, what are you lookin' for?' I started at the sound of Jed's voice and he stood in the doorway, looking from her to me, his eyes hard with suspicion. My face flamed. I felt like a kid at a peepshow. He was the only brother I had and I had been looking at his daughter in a way that could have got me killed.

Maybe he hadn't noticed. He seemed to be concentrating on Salena. She looked at him awkwardly, aware of something wrong, not knowing what. 'I found Mister Saul in here, looking for something to drink. He has a bad stomach.'

It was too much. I sat down at the table and buried my burning face in my hands and Jed said, 'Go back to bed. I know what Saul wants.' I heard her go and then he came around to me and put a hand on my shoulder.

I muttered, 'It ain't my stomach.'

'I know. One of the things I heard was you was drunk most of the time. I guess it's been hard, tryin' to stop.'

I raised my head, 'You'll never know.'

'I got something in my bedroom. I keep it for medicine because I can't afford to make it a habit. You're welcome to it.'

He left and came back with a small whisky bottle, half full. 'Not enough to ease your pain, Saul, but it might help for tonight.' He held it out to me.

I saw my hands tremble as I reached for it and I was sick with self loathing, but I couldn't have stopped myself if my life depended on it. I uncorked the bottle and tilted it to my lips and took several deep gulps of the firewater and suddenly everything was easy again. I put down the bottle on the table in front of me and swore at it and Jed stood back in the shadows watching me.

At last I summoned up the guts to look at him. 'Jed,' I said softly, 'I guess you'll never know just how low I've been.'

He shook his head and his eyes were warm with sympathy, 'You got cause.'

'You better leave me alone, now,' I said.

He nodded and went, leaving me in that little pool of light with that tiny amount of amber liquid sparkling in the bottom of the bottle, the most important thing in the world to me. I rose slowly, turned out the lamp and went back to bed, taking the bottle with me. I lay there having the smallest sips of the dregs in the bottle, making them last, till there was no more, then, like a child cuddling his favourite toy, I fell asleep, hugging the empty bottle to my breast.

CHAPTER THREE

JED had gone when I rose in the morning and there was no sign of Salena, so I fixed myself some coffee for that was all I wanted and took it in to Tilda's room.

She was awake and sitting up, freshly tended and I sat on the edge of the bed and drank my coffee and talked to her a while. When silence fell between us, she stirred a little then asked, 'You feelin' better this mornin', boy?'

I avoided her eyes, 'Who said I was sick?'

'Salena.'

I looked at her then and her black, wrinkled face was innocent. I guessed she didn't know the truth.

'I think I was a mite tired, with the journey and all.'

'That's what I said it was.' She seemed satisfied and I didn't press any more information on her.

'Where's Jed?'

'Out in the fields, but he has to take the buggy to town later to fetch some provisions for Miz Bowen. Whyn't you take a ride in with him?'

'I will,' I said, rising. 'I meant to bring you something when I came but I didn't manage it. I'll find something for you and Salena in town, I guess.'

'You're not to spend your money on me, Saul, you hear?' But her voice held pleasure. She didn't get too many presents.

I grinned, 'I got more than I need.'

Later, I went looking for Jed and found him in one of the stables, harnessing a horse to a small wagon. He waved a greeting at me.

'Tilda said you're going to town. Mind if I join you?'

'You're welcome.' He made no mention of the night before, so I leaned against a post, watching him.

I said, 'I owe you a bottle of medicine.'

He looked up, the questioning shadowing his eyes. 'You sure you want to pay it back?'

I knew what he meant. 'Jed, I got to be able to go in there and get a bottle and not touch what's in it. I got to. You understand?'

He nodded, 'Don't fret about it.'

I said, 'I'm shamed. I really am.'

'No need to be.'

He was finished and I saw him fumble in his vest pocket and pull out a crumpled list and study it, then replace it. 'I'm ready,' he said at last, 'Come on up.'

He climbed into the wagon and took up the reins and I got in beside him. The horse moved out of the stable into the sunshine of the yard and I blinked in the sudden brilliance and pulled my hat brim low over my eyes to shade them.

Once out of sight of the ranch I settled down and relaxed. Jed didn't say much, humming some tune to himself, and I kept my eyes on the horse's moving hindquarters and the swish of its tail while my mind wandered, pondering just what I hoped to achieve on this visit when I had failed on all the others. Last night's meeting with Abe showed things were just the same where he was concerned and I couldn't blame him. Deep down, it concerned me that though I had meant it when I told Jed I had to prove I could touch a bottle and not drink from it, even so, when I had gone to my bags to take out the money for Tilda's and Salena's gifts and the whisky I owed Jed, I had taken out far more than I needed, in case. In case of what? In case I couldn't stand by my brave words? Already I was half-way to not proving a thing and I knew it.

Jed's humming broke off and he said, 'Here's a place don't change much.'

I looked up and around me. We had already entered the town and he was right. It was almost the same as when I had last seen it. There was the sheriff's office and the jail, two stores and the restaurant and the saloon all needing painting, streaked with wind and weather, faded by sun, bustling with false importance. It was near noon and as we passed the saloon I heard the voices and smelled the fumes that issued from the batwing doors and I tightened my dry mouth and turned my head away, feeling the fresh stomach cramps twist me inside.

Jed drew up at the General Store. He hitched the horse and I joined him on the boardwalk. He said, 'I got some things to do. You have yourself a look around and I'll come find you when I'm done.'

I nodded and left him and walked away, hearing my boot-heels on the planking as loud as if I were alone though folks passed me all the time. There were one or two familiar faces that stared at me in sudden recognition and open curiosity, but I ignored them. I did not know their names and did not care, though maybe once I had. At a carved fountain on a street corner I paused and dipped my hands in the cool water and splashed it over my face. My skin felt taut and dry and the dampness helped a little. I cupped my hands, filling them, and drank, then moved on.

Further down Main there was a new store. It said, over the entrance, 'Ladies' Gowns'. I looked in the window at the three calico dresses on display. They were plain and cheap but I could see past them into the dim recesses of the shop where a shelf carried ribbons and shoe boxes and jewellery. I opened the door and went in. The woman behind the counter looked up from her customer in curiosity and the elderly woman she was serving turned too. I knew her, but couldn't remember where I had seen her. Her look was one of sudden recognition and I could plainly see the distaste on her respectable face.

I thought wryly of what must be my reputation in this small town, then dismissed the thought and moved over to look at the trinkets I had seen from the window. I chose a necklace each for Tilda and Salena and made the woman behind the counter add some Eau de Cologne to Tilda's package and some ribbons to Salena's. She looked up at me from time to time as she wrapped the parcels and she was young and homely and there was bright hope in her eyes. When I paid her she tossed back her hair from her forehead and thrust out her flat chest, so when I took the change from her I gave her a warm look and let my fingers brush the back of her hand so that her cheeks went dark and hot. It raised some devil in me to give her a little pleasure for she was an obvious spinster. Before the door closed behind me I heard the sudden excited whisper of gossip from the other customer who had watched me all the time I had been in the shop.

Crossing the street, I walked back on the other side, carrying my parcels under my arm. I licked my lower lip nervously as I neared the saloon, I knew what I had to do and knew, too, what I probably would do. I pushed the batwing doors and they swung shut behind me. It was cool in there and dark. The reek of alcohol stung in my nostrils and my throat burned dry. Only a few glanced up as I moved towards the bar, and some I knew and some were strangers. The murmur of conversation flowed around me as I leaned on the bar, waiting.

'What'll you have?' The bartender moved towards me, frowning a little, wondering where he had seen me before.

'A small bottle of whisky. Scotch.'

'You want to drink it here?' He was still puzzling.

'No.' I hardly heard the word, my voice seemed strange and far away. The bartender shrugged and turned and reached up to a shelf. I saw the bottles standing there, all shapes, all sizes. He reached one and brought it to me.

'It's the best we've got,' he squinted at me. 'Costs plenty.'

'I know,' I said, the strangeness still in my voice. I took out some silver and paid him and his fingers closed over the money. He began to move away.

'Wait,' I said.

The bartender stopped and looked back at me and I thought I must have looked pale and tense. 'Get me another bottle, a large one this time, and a glass.'

He nodded, a flicker in his eyes, and reached for another bottle, twice the size of the first. I paid him again, picked up the two bottles and the glass and turned to find a table.

The bartender's voice reached me through a haze. 'I remember you. You're Saul Bowen, ain't you?'

I looked at him, feeling the smile crooked on my lips. 'That's right.'

His eyes hooded, 'You been gone a long time.'

'Uh huh.'

His gaze fell to the bottles in my grasp, 'No trouble,' he said softly, 'Not like last time.'

'I dis-remember.'

'Likely. You were too drunk.'

'Did I pay you?'

'After a while.'

'Then you got no complaints.' I moved away to a table and sat down and put my parcels and the bottles on it, in front of me. It was Jed's small bottle that I opened first and that drink burned like fire, raw and breathtaking. I tossed back the contents of the glass and poured out another and drank it in a gulp. There were some who had begun to stare by the time I had finished the fourth and the conversation became muted and awed as the level of liquid moved steadily down the bottle. There were comings and goings and I stayed there, sober as a judge, drinking more slowly and none interfered or spoke to me, recognising, I guess, a man who was going to drink himself blind no matter the consequences.

It was well into the afternoon and I kept my eyes on the floorboards beside my table. They were marked and in a little while I could see strange faces and patterns in the stains. I felt cool and steady, but the faces on the floor began to writhe and twirl in a senseless dance. I don't know when it was that I opened the second bottle, but that was when I began to feel bad. Maybe I should have been sick, and one day, I thought, it'll kill me, but I had been doing it for a long time and I guess I could hold more than most. Soon, I knew, the bad feeling would pass away and I'd feel good, warm and happy and then sweet darkness would take over.

It was evening then, I guess, for everything was shadowed. The pale sunbeams from the window lay long on the floor and dust motes danced in them, round and round, making me dizzy. I couldn't see too well and people moved around me in a haze of twilit shapes, but I had been deaf to them for some time. There was a pain in my stomach and I took another drink to still it. Now it was the time for me to feel good; no pain, no grief, no guilt, just me and the bottle and, soon, sleep.

But they wouldn't let it come. There was a weight on my shoulder, a hand squeezing and shaking. I blinked and squinted, not able to make out who it was, irritated at the persistence of it. I swore, my voice thick and mumbling and pushed away the hand. It came back, trying to bring me to my feet. I reached for what was left in the whisky bottle and it was moved out of my reach. That riled me, I guess, and I took a clumsy swing at whoever was leaning over me. A voice throbbed at me, calling me by name, telling me to move. I lashed out again and felt flesh under my fist and lost my balance as it moved out of range. The floor came up and hit me and the whirling floorboards were hard and unyielding. Then the darkness came.

There was an uncomfortable jolting under me when I awoke, and something coarse and lumpy was under my cheek. It smelled of sacking and flour and foodstuffs and made me sick to my stomach. High overhead the stars wheeled by and the occasional black branches of a tree, silhouetted in the evening sky. I was covered by a blanket and I was lying in the bottom of the wagon. I rolled over and tried to sit up and my whole body cried out in protest. The stale taste of whisky and vomit filled my mouth and my stomach churned. I could see Jed's back sitting high in the driver's seat and I said thickly, 'Stop, Jed. I got to get out.'

He pulled up and turned to look down at me, his face black in the shadows. I put both hands on the tail gate and tried to climb over it, but had no strength so that I lost my balance and tumbled over it, hitting the hard-packed trail with a jolt that tore the breath from my body. That made me sick again, lying there, and Jed came around and helped me to my feet. He said, 'You done?'

I nodded weakly. I could see his mouth was puffy and there was a cut on the corner of it. I mumbled, 'What happened to you?'

He said, 'You didn't want to come home.'

I shook my head, 'Didn't prove a thing, did I?'

'Nope.'

Whether or not he was disgusted, he didn't show it. Expressionlessly, he helped me back into the wagon and I lay there quietly, sleeping on and off, till we pulled up at last outside Aunt Tilda's shack.

CHAPTER FOUR

In the morning I awoke to the long accustomed throb in my temples and the thickness of a tongue, dry and furred, clinging to the roof of my mouth so I almost choked. There was a deep gnawing at my guts.

The sun was high and very bright so it was well into the morning and I could hear the far-off voices of the workers in the pastures and larks singing out in the high blue. There was no sound of movement in the house so I guessed Jed and Salena were away and that Tilda was asleep. I rolled over and stifled a groan as the pain slammed against my skull at the movement. I rose and went into the kitchen and worked the pump and put my hand under the fresh, cold jet of water. It hurt. Even my teeth and my ears protested.

'Saul,' It was Tilda's old-woman's quaver.

I took a little time answering, spitting out water and smoothing back my hair, then I turned and made my way to her room. The door was open. I leaned against the jamb because the fierce pain in my stomach refused to let me stand straight. I needed another drink badly, just one to set me straight.

'Yes, ma'am?' I tried not to notice the hurt in her eyes.

'How you feelin', boy?'

I looked away, 'I'll live.'

'Jed tried to tell me you was sick again. I know what sickness it was, I could smell it from here.' Her voice dropped and when I looked back at her, she was holding out her hand. 'Come here, Saul.' Some devil in me held me back and clamped my tongue. 'I know men get drunk and you're a man full-growed. Why try to hide it from me? I'm too old to be shocked.' Her hand fell and lay dark and still on the white coverlet.

I said, 'Did Jed bring the parcels?' my voice sounding false and strange.

Her face changed, betraying her disappointment in me. 'In there, somewhere.'

'I got something for you,' I forced a smile, 'I'll go find it.'

The small packages from the dress shop were on a shelf in the kitchen and beside them stood the half-empty bottle of whisky from the night before. Guiltily, I reached for it, unscrewed the cork and took a long pull at the contents. My head swam and tears came to my eyes and I couldn't restrain a cough, but it made me feel just a mite better. I put back the bottle, brought down the packages and went back to Tilda.

' 'Tain't much, but I hope you know how I feel for you.' I handed her a parcel. 'The pearls and ribbons in the other one are for Salena.'

Tilda's crabbed old hands shook and she had difficulty undoing the parcel. I didn't offer to do it for her, my own hands were trembling more than hers. I drew my fingers across my mouth and licked my lips, feeling the yearning grow.

She said nothing, holding up the cheap, green glass beads. They sparkled, a Christmas bauble, in the shafts of yellow sunlight that streamed from the window. A tear dropped from her chin and I looked away and said, 'I can afford better but there's no choice in town.'

'I know. I know what you're trying to say.'

I rose, 'I'll go find Jed. See does he want any help.'

It was almost a relief to get away from there, away from the fresh guilt that clamoured in me. Jed was supervising a crew that was cutting and stacking hay for winter feed for the animals. A part of Abe's success, I guess, was that he was self-supporting. There was enough land to grow the horses' feed; and he had his own horse-breakers and his own blacksmith. Jed saw me watching them and, as though reading my mind, he handed me a pitchfork saying, 'You want to throw in with us, there's plenty of work.'

I set to, willingly, far too hard and fast for a man who had wasted so much time. I was out of condition and tired easily, while the sweat burst from me and soaked through my clothes. But the bad taste and the pain and the sick feeling rolled out too, replaced by the clean, sore goodness of hard work. I stopped at noon and ate and drank with the men and though they didn't have much to say to me, they didn't have much to say to each other. We were one team, understanding and co-operating with no need for words and for a while I almost forgot who and what I was. The work went on until it was almost dark, and we dispersed, going our separate ways.

I went back towards Tilda's place, aching in every bone, feeling the cool twilight breeze drying the perspiration on my back and in my armpits. The grove of trees loomed up on my left, and because I felt a little more worthy, I guess, I veered towards it and the pale wash of white marble that I could see gleaming in patches through the interlacing tangle of lower branches. I stood for a while, silent, under a sad old oak before I approached my mother's grave.

I stood two feet away, looking over the elaborate memorial that Abe had had made. There was an image of my mother, raised in cameo, on the headstone and underneath it were the gold-lettered words 'In memory of Sarah Bowen, beloved wife of Abe. Forced from this life, June 1879'. There was no mention of me, I had already ceased to exist. I felt my face twist with the awful pain that always clutched me when I came here. I should stay away, but there was a kind of penance, an appeasement in admitting my guilt here at the place where she rested. I put out my hand to touch the cold, hard lines of her carved profile and, as usual, the feel of it trembled through the tips of my fingers like a shock. My hand shook a little as I drew it away and suddenly I looked up and beyond the grave.

Something or someone was standing under the far trees, looking at me, pale in the deepening dusk. The figure was still, white clad, the breeze playing a little with the tendrils of yellow hair that swept over her face. Wild lilies drooped a little in the silvery arms and there seemed to be a light glow surrounding the quiet figure. My mouth dried and something lurched deep in my stomach. I felt the strong bile of fear rise in my throat and I almost cried out. All these years I had expected it, and now she had come. I wanted to cry out but I was as petrified as the grave stone.

The figure moved then, took a step towards me, then

another, and I saw the stranger's lips move in a stranger's smile, small, hesitating, and the terror left me, leaving me weak, anger replacing it at the thought I may have betrayed my feelings.

She said, lisping slightly, 'Saul? Are you Saul?'

I said nothing, still faint with the remnants of my emotion.

'I'm sorry if I startled you.' My father's wife advanced towards me, the lilies she carried trembling across her arm. 'I brought flowers. For the grave.' Her voice was deep, lightly and attractively accented, but I could say nothing, struck dumb by her resemblance to that other I had loved, remembering and agonised by the memory.

A small shadow crossed her grey eyes and I sensed her uncertainty as she went to her knees and laid the pale lilies across the grave. The pale hair tumbled about her face and shoulders as she bowed her head a moment and then she rose, looking at me, her nervousness apparently gone, her eyes frank and friendly. 'I heard you were here at the ranch. I wished to meet you.'

I found my voice, 'You're Abe's new wife.' The words came out flat and harsh and she blanched a little.

'I hope you don't mind.'

'None of my business.'

She flinched again and I would have felt pity if I hadn't hated her so. She was pretty and young; too young for Abe.

'I think it is.' Was that defiance I detected in her words? Good, I wanted her to fight, I could fight too, dirtier than she knew.

'What Abe does is his affair. Don't make no never mind to me.' I added, spitefully, 'My Ma's been gone a long time.' And then, in spite of myself, I blurted, 'You look like her.'

I don't know how she felt about that, whether she wanted to know or not. Something crossed her face and then she came to me and held out her hand, 'But my name is Ilse. Will you call me Ilse?'

I ignored her hand, 'If I ever have to call you anything, I guess.'

I recognised the hurt in her eyes. I had seen it too often

before with women I knew, beginning with my mother. She dropped her hand and used it to smooth down her dress, giving it something to do, I suppose. She said softly, 'Please don't resent me, Saul. I want to be your friend.'

That was funny. I gave a short bark of laughter, 'And stay married to Abe?'

Shock hit her. I heard her breath go in and catch. 'He is your father!' Protest in her cry.

'Tell him that,' I turned to go and made a step away.

'Saul,' She reached and put a hand on my arm, stopping me. 'I don't understand. This enmity, I don't understand. Why are you both like this?'

I stared into her eyes looking for lies and finding only guilelessness. 'Ask him. You'll understand then.'

I moved away again and this time she didn't try to stop me.

Salena waited on us at supper-time, fresh and young and pretty. Aunt Tilda wasn't feeling too good and I sat with her a while. She made no mention of the night before and I was more than glad to talk of other things. We reminisced together of years gone by and I tried not to let it hurt too much to remember my childhood. She had done her best for me and, for one, she had enjoyed those days, loving me and being sentimental about the things I had done, how bright I had been, laughing a little with her eyes dark and wet with pride even over my 'orneriness', as she called it. I listened and laughed and was grateful and loved her too, burying the memories until I had left her and was alone, in the darkness, lying on top of my bed, smoking, one arm flung up under the back of my head and seeing things the way they really had been, not the way Tilda liked to think they were, fooling herself, not me.

I hadn't forgotten those times, playing with Jed, tagging after him even after he had grown up and away from me, making him the brother I had never had; knowing their home was my home and staring, uselessly, over at the Big House, knowing I could never enter it again, the sense of loss hiding but eating ever deeper into my very being. Sometimes Abe would come out on to the porch and I would stand still.

looking at his tall, formidable figure, aching for some sign of recognition, a look, a tiny stirring of interest, but he would gaze straight through me as though I were invisible, non-existent, and it penetrated, gradually, that I was non-existent, that I was nothing, had never been anything. Deep down, as with all children, I never lost hope and at night, I dreamed, again and again, that he was speaking to me, that he was pleased and that he smiled. And when I woke I hated him and wished that he would hate me too, even that was better than being ignored.

I rose impatiently and went to the window and threw out my cigarette, watching its red arc in the darkness. Raising my eyes, I could see the black bulk of the Big House, only one of its windows lighted, golden with the gentle glow of an oil lamp. It was the bedroom window and I wondered if she were in there, Ilse, talking to Abe, perhaps mentioning her meeting with me. I guessed she had not been too impressed. She was probably telling Abe he was right to ignore me. I was rude and arrogant and unco-operative. So what the hell?

I paced up and down, the familiar burning ache eating my guts, wanting that damn bottle of Jed's, knowing where it was and exactly how much was in it. By God, I needed it. So I had bought it for him to replace the one I emptied, but he didn't need it right now, it was for medicine. I could always get him another one, take another trip into town. I'd go in the morning. I opened the door and went into the kitchen. There was enough moonlight to see the jars and bottles on the shelf and I took down the whisky bottle with what was left in it glinting a little. The feel of it was warm and friendly and comforting. It was good just to have my fingers curl around the neck of the bottle. I took it with me into the bedroom and lay on the bed, still fully dressed, and drank myself to sleep again.

CHAPTER FIVE

JED was gone when I awoke the next morning. It was still early and I had the feeling he had left deliberately to avoid seeing me. Couldn't bear to, I guess. Knowing the way I was, the first thing he would have done was look for the whisky, and seeing it gone I thought his disgust had probably been too much for him to have even looked at me. I didn't blame him.

Somehow, I had stilled my trembling hands enough to wash and shave and change my rumpled shirt. I gritted my teeth and made a bold front for Aunt Tilda who called her good mornings from her room, unsuspecting. I felt obliged to Jed for not having told her anything. He was a better man than I could ever hope to be.

I couldn't face eating anything, so I was glad Salena was over at the Big House, cleaning. She would have fussed and made me a breakfast and I couldn't have explained how it was that I could never eat after drinking. Soon enough I left the cottage, looking for Jed and something to do. My stomach was starting to act up again and I had to be moving. I found him at last with a cluster of hands, bending over a foal that had been hooked on wire and had torn a gash in its chest. I heard him say, 'Not as bad as it looks. It'll scar some,' and someone else answered, 'Do the best you can, Jed. We'll lose money on it, else.'

He said, 'Yessir,' and Abe straightened and looked me full in the face. His brows drew together momentarily in that scarce hidden displeasure, then his face cleared and went cold and distant. He sent a small nod in my direction then turned on his heel and walked away. I stared after him, my heart pounding as usual with whatever churned me inside when he was near.

Jed threw a look my way, 'You want to do something, we're rounding up the foals been runnin' in the south pasture. Some of them have been staked and they'll need cleaning up like this 'un. You and that gelding willing to throw in a hand?'

I said, 'Sure,' and went to fetch the black.

It was a hard morning's work, and hot. Those damn mares did all their running in the sun, avoiding the cool shade of the trees around the stream that watered Abe's southern pastures. I was stale and missed too often with the rope and found myself wondering what the other hands were thinking. They said nothing as their ropes settled over the shoulders of some mare that I had been chasing, red-faced and sweating, for too long. The gelding had no cow sense and I had lost mine over the years, dulled with drink and other sins. I was no help at all and would have been better away from them, I told myself as my stomach knotted again.

Jed avoided me, and I knew he was thinking of that missing bottle. I guess I would rather have had him come out with it and show his disgust, but he just withdrew his support, involving himself only with the other hands, joshing one and quietly planning some sensible move with another, working out how to avoid spooking some particularly skittish mare who was showing signs of wanting to lead them a good dance before she gave up her foal for their unwanted ministrations. In a while, I slowed down the lathered gelding and walked him quietly down to the stream and let him drink. I took up a handful of dry grass and rubbed him down, taking off the white foam on his neck and flanks, watching the dark coat turn blacker with the moisture on it.

No one was watching me, each engrossed in his own business, so I remounted and rode away quickly, out of the pasture, heading for the shack. Once I turned to look back and saw Jed in the distance. He had stopped and was looking after me. I thought if he should raise his hand or make some sign, I'd go back and try again, but he turned and moved his horse back to work, bored with me and my problems. So I moved on.

Back at the cottage, I put money into my pockets, remounted the gelding and left the ranch, feeling bad, yet good too. Each step away from Abe's place lightened my heart and eased my guilt. I was glad I had made my decision. I had chosen a path of my own making and who were Jed, or Aunt Tilda or anyone else to deny me the right to follow it. They had no right. With new determination I put spurs to the gelding's hide and he snorted with distaste for action, but he moved faster, reluctantly.

It was quiet in town, at midday, with no one on the boardwalk, but there were sounds coming from the saloon and I headed there quickly, emptying myself of all feeling except the one important one that was my main motivation these days. My mouth was dry with thirst and it was a good enough excuse. I tethered the gelding and went in.

Four old men played a game of poker at one of the tables, half empty beer bottles at their elbows and smeared glasses before them. Two tired looking cowhands stood at the bar, staring straight ahead, grim-faced and silent as they drank slowly from glasses of golden amber, the very sight of which made me ache.

The barkeep's eyes narrowed as he caught sight of me. I crossed the floor and sat on one of the stools at the bar.

He said, 'You again.'

I raised my hands placatingly, 'My money's good.'

'Can't deny that,' I knew he wished I was broke and a bum so that he'd have some excuse to throw me out. 'A Bowen's money's always good.'

I took out some silver, 'That's for whisky. No redeye, your best.'

He nodded wearily, 'The best.' He turned to fetch a glass. Beside me, the two cowboys looked me over carefully.

One said, 'The best don't make you drunk any quicker.'

His friend shook his head, 'Maybe not, but it don't rot your guts so bad, Tolley.'

The barkeep brought me a glass of the good Scotch he kept up on the shelf and I nodded. 'Stay around,' I said.

'Got no place else to go.' He sounded weary as though he wished he had somewhere else to spend the afternoon. Maybe he sensed trouble.

Tolley and his friend studied me in the mirror behind the

bar as I took a small sip, then tossed back the rest of the Scotch. I didn't care whether or not they stared. I put down the glass, feeling good. 'I'll have another,' I told the barkeep. He stopped polishing glasses with his grimy rag and bent to refill my glass.

Tolley said, 'Rots your guts whether it's good whisky or bad, friend, you drink enough of it.'

His companion said, 'Or drink it fast enough.'

They watched me in silence as I rolled another mouthful around my gums and swallowed. In the mirror my eyes met theirs. Deliberately, I drank the second glassful almost at a toss.

'Ever tasted real good whisky, Tolley?'

'Once, a while back. Mighty friendly kind of a man bought me a drink.'

'That was right neighbourly.'

'Right neighbourly,' agreed Tolley.

They were needling me and I knew it. They probably knew who I was by reputation. Most people did, it seemed. I called the barkeep again. 'Sell me the rest of that bottle,' I caught the cowboys' eyes in the mirror. 'It's good stuff and good stuff is hard to get.'

He shrugged, resigned, and put the bottle on top of the bar. I paid him, took up the bottle and glass and turned to take my reason for living to a table. As I came near Tolley I said, 'I always believed when a man wanted to get good and drunk on his lonesome, he should be allowed to do it,' and moved away and sat down.

Their backs went rigid, but I wasn't caring now. This was where I belonged and where I knew my way around, right now to the bottom of that bottle. But I hoped I'd never see the bottom of it. Comforting oblivion should have enveloped me long before then. I set to work to hasten its onset.

Sometime during the afternoon and half-way down my bottle, a girl came into the saloon. She was no lady but one of the saloon girls. I didn't know her but she seemed to know me, stopping beside me and smiling a little before she went to join Tolley and his friend at the bar. They whooped when they saw her and each put an arm around her waist, pulling her first against one and then the other, 'Hey, Abbie!'

'Abbie, what'll you have?'

'Where you been, Abbie? Thought you weren't comin.'

I heard her giggle, it rolled around in my fuzzy head. 'I'll have beer, Tolley darlin'. Now you shouldn't have waited on me, you know it's my time off.' I saw the blur of her face as she turned it towards me, momentarily, then she returned her attention to them.

'Honey, I'm always waiting to catch a sight of you. Why, you're the best thing around here, you know that and you're my special girl.'

'How long have I been Tolley's girl?' She sounded surprised.

'Why, honey, you remember! Last week, you remember?'

'You got paid last week.'

'I still got some left, Abbie honey.'

'It don't last with you, Tolley. I can't afford you.' There was a smile in her voice, but the bite of truth came into my befuddled head. My bottle clinked against my glass and again, from the corner of my eye, I saw the white blur of her face directed towards me. Their voices rolled in my head, meaningless, not affecting me. Let them talk. My belly was warm and tingling and I was happy. Old Man Whisky was my home, Old Man Whisky was my Pa. I tasted him and loved him as he did good things to me. Come on, old man, another sip of your fine, warm body—and then she was beside me, her hand covering mine. She was saying something and it annoyed me. Why couldn't she leave me alone? I was better off alone, hurting no one. 'Come on,' her voice came into my head, 'I know you. I've heard all about you and I'll just bet you're friendly, Mister Saul Bowen. I'll bet you're real friendly.'

Someone else joined her, someone whose voice grated on my nerves, 'Friendly as hell!'

She snapped, 'Shut up!' and the sharpness of her tone hurt my head. I said, 'Hush.'

'Spare a drink, huh, Mister Bowen? Just one little drink for me. I can be real grateful.'

I moved her hand off mine deliberately. It was the only thing I could see, her white hand resting on mine in the gloom and it was heavy. I could hardly refill my glass. I wondered if she were pretty and squinted my eyes, trying to see her face. I mouthed, 'Abbie?' and she wriggled, 'Oh gee, you know my name.'

It was Tolley who stood behind her. He bent over her shoulder, looking at me with hostility. I blinked, trying to focus on his face. 'You wasting your time off, Abbie. I'm willing and I'm sober,' Tolley muttered.

I saw her push at him with her shoulder, 'Tolley, you're broke. I know it.'

He pushed her back and I snatched at my precious bottle as it swayed on the table, steadying it. Tolley yelled, 'You'll get nothing from a drunk like that!' and she screeched at him.

The noise went through my head and I roared, then Tolley was coming at me. His weight hit me and we crashed to the ground, my chair under me. I heard my breath leave my body with an audible sound and Tolley's hands were on my shoulders, forcing me down. Lights flashed in front of my eyes and I heard the crash of glass as my whisky bottle hit the ground and smashed. I lost my temper. I was drunk, but I had been drunker and more helpless. The girl called Abbie kept yelling and Tolley was swearing, so I heaved him from me bodily and he disappeared from sight. I began to scramble to my hands and knees. Then Tolley came back into view. He was standing and he had my half full glass in his hands and he tossed back the contents at one gulp, glaring at me defiantly. It was all I had left, now, I was kneeling in the spilled pool on the floor, so I flung myself at Tolley's knees. He went down with a shout and I heard the glass splinter. Tolley hit the table as he fell and it skidded and turned on its side as we rolled against it. There was wetness on my face as Tolley clawed at me and I saw red splashed on his vest front. There was yelling all around, the girl's voice and other men and someone was tugging at the back of my collar. A deep voice said, 'Stop it, Bowen. I said stop it!'

I shook my head and punched at Tolley's lopsided misty

face and took a fist from him, high on the side of the jaw then I was dragged to my feet like some idiot puppy and held upright. Something heavy settled around my wrist and a vice-like grip held the other. The deep voice said, 'Hold him, hold his arm!' and I kicked out at whoever spoke, a big, black shape in the dimness of drunkenness and late afternoon. I connected and there was a pained grunt, then another steel band encircled my other wrist and I was shackled.

I spat, standing still at last. Gradually, the haze cleared. At my feet sat Tolley, groaning and holding his glass-slashed, blood-dripping hand. There was redness soaking his shirt and mine too. The girl stood to one side, big-eyed, staring at me in some sort of excitement. The man who held me was tall, dark, heavy-moustached and humourless. He wore a star on his black vest. He shook me as though I were a small boy, his strong fingers still clutching the back of my collar. 'You're trouble, Bowen. Always were, always will be. You'll kill your old man, some day. Clean break his heart!' He shook me again, and God help me, I threw up. Right there at his feet.

It was the last straw. He marched me out of there, muttering between his teeth and my feet hardly touched the ground.

As we raced down the street, I tried to remember his name and failed. I guess one hundred yards was never covered so fast. I was through the sheriff's office door, across the floor and into a cell before I could draw breath, though that was difficult enough with his choking grip on my collar. He released me and I fell on my side on the stone floor and I heard the clang of the barred doors and the key grated in the lock as I raised myself painfully on one elbow as best I could with the manacles locked tight on my wrists.

He gritted, 'Now cool off!' and went quickly away, back to his office slamming the door behind him and leaving me on my own in the cell. I came awkwardly to my feet and made my way over to the cot that stood against one wall and lay down on its hard, striped mattress. There was a red blanket neatly folded at the foot of the bed and I shook it out, drew it over my shoulders and tried to sleep. I could hear sounds outside, horses in the street and footsteps, and there were flies buzzing in my cell. After a while, all the sounds merged soothingly and I did sleep.

It was dark when I awoke to the jangling of keys, but I started to shake a little from the effects of the drinking and from the lack of more of what I needed, so I stayed still, letting whoever entered come up to me. It was a deputy. He shook my shoulder and said, 'Here, trouble, eat something. There's coffee, too.' I opened one eye and saw him put a covered tray on the floor beside the cot. He stood and put his hands on his hips, staring down at me. 'Move it, feller. Your folks is comin' to git you. Though why in hell they want to beats me.'

I opened both eyes and struggled to sit, forgetting the manacles on my hands. They sounded metallically and cut short my effort to raise myself on my elbow. 'Folks?' My head pounded and my eyes felt red and gritty, 'Which folks?'

The deputy snapped, 'Miz Bowen, I guess. Who else?' He turned and looked at me over his shoulder, 'You sure are a pretty sight. I wouldn't like to admit you was kin of mine.' He opened the cell door and shut and locked it after him. I didn't want the stew that steamed in a bowl on the tray. It required too much effort to use the spoon when I was shackled that way. Besides, the look and smell of it made me sick to my stomach. But I drank the coffee. It was strong and black and helped my head just a little.

Someone had lit a lamp in the passageway outside the cell door and I lay and looked at it after I finished my coffee. I didn't believe the deputy's statement that Ilse was coming. Why should she? And I hoped to God she wasn't. I did not want her to see me this way, though I didn't know why I cared. The sheriff had probably sent word back to the ranch and I guessed old Jed would have had to be the one to fetch me home. Poor Jed, I had to admit he was probably cursing the day I had come home.

I lay there for close on another hour before I heard voices and footsteps and then they came. It was Ilse and Jed and the sheriff and they stood looking at me before the sheriff put his key in the lock and flung open the cell door. 'All right,

Bowen, you're free to go.' His voice was dry with distaste. Slowly, I moved back the blanket and sat up, hating to see the expression in Jed's and Ilse's faces as they stared at my rumpled, blood-stained clothes and my obviously haggard, pain-etched face. I drew the back of my hand across my mouth, hearing the chain-links clink and feeling the beard stubble on my chin, then came unsteadily to my feet. I stumbled a little making my way over to them and avoided their eyes while the sheriff unlocked the manacles. He tucked them into his belt and said to me, 'I don't want to see you in here again, understand? But, by God, you cause any more trouble in this town and this is where you'll be and for a damn sight longer. You hear me, feller?' He was staring into my eyes petulantly, itching for a hostile reaction from me, I guess. But all I did was murmur, 'I hear,' and I felt rather than saw the disgust in him.

Ilse turned to him. She said, 'Thank you, sheriff. I appreciate this. You do understand, don't you, that I think it is unnecessary for Mr Bowen to hear about this? There is no point in causing him any further worry.' Her voice was soft and pretty and persuasive and the sheriff looked at her with scarcely concealed admiration. I didn't blame him, if I had had any sense I would have realised just how beautiful and generous she was, and how genuine—but I felt only resentment. She was a newcomer and had no idea of what drove me and made me this way. Not understanding, she set herself up in my mother's place taking over and ruling me as though I were a child. Someday, I told myself, someday soon I'd set her on her ears, the prissy do-gooder. I thought this standing next to Jed and glaring at her with animosity, while the sheriff said, 'Yes, ma'am. I'll see it doesn't get around,' and she smiled and simpered up at him. Maybe my feelings showed on my face, Jed caught my eye and gave his head a small shake, his features set and angry and my enmity turned to him. Hating both of them, I left the sheriff's office and climbed awkwardly into the buggy. My gelding was tethered behind and it followed as we went through dimly lit Main Street and took the trail for home.

Ilse spoke only once on the journey and that was addressed across me to Jed. She said, 'Remember, Jed, if Abe asks you, that I had to visit Mrs Olsen. Her time is near.'

Jed nodded, 'Sure, ma'am.' He clucked to the horse and it speeded its gait, dragging my gelding, head out thrust, behind the vehicle.

At the ranch, Jed stopped only momentarily outside Aunt Tilda's cottage, time enough to let me climb down, then he drove on quickly, with Ilse, to the Big House. I didn't stop to watch them light, but went in quickly, hoping Salena would not be in the kitchen. She was, I moved past her, head down, but I heard her gasp before I went into my room and closed the door.

I sat on the bed awhile and rolled a cigarette with shaking fingers and smoked, but started to feel sick again, so I put it out and went to the washstand and poured water from the jug into a bowl and washed, delighting in the fresh coolness on my tired, puffy skin. I took a clean shirt from the drawer and changed, feeling better and had the courage, at last, to look at myself in the mirror. I was a mess. What any woman could see in me I didn't know. My eyes were red, my skin stretched taut with strain, an unhealthy yellowish pallor on my cheeks and blue stubble showing on my chin. The dark hair, damp with sweat, hung over my forehead, shadowing those deep eyes that had been to hell and back and would go there again, soon as I needed to.

I was standing there when I heard Jed's voice in the kitchen and then he knocked at my door and came in. He stood staring at me as I leaned with my hands on the washstand still looking at my reflection. At last I said, 'Don't say it, Jed. I know.' Not wanting to see him.

'Do you?' His voice was tight, 'You know what you owe that lady today? You can thank God Abe was out when the sheriff came. Miz Bowen got the message and made her arrangements.'

I began to get mad. 'Who asked for her help? What's she trying to do? Be some kind of a go-between with Abe and me? Can't she get it into her thick skull that it's no good and never will be?'

Jed was silent a moment, but I could see the expressions chase over his face, pity, contempt and disappointment. 'Why don't you give her a chance, Saul? Maybe she'll be the way for you to sort out things with your Pa,' he said quietly at last.

'Who asked her?' I snapped again. 'Tell her to keep her nose out of my business. I don't need her and I ain't thankin' her.' I felt a fool and could sense my control of events slipping away, that's what hurt.

Annoyance showed in Jed, 'You made your bed, Saul. I don't have much patience with you any more.' He was shutting me out, exhausted with me, and he had every right. I knew I would lose him too, like I lost everyone who mattered and I stood and watched him slip away, sick and sorry as hell and my tongue shaped the words, 'It was a mistake coming back here. I've seen Tilda and I'm glad for that. As for the rest of this place, I ain't interested in it. I'll get out tomorrow. There's things to do and places to see I haven't got around to doing and seeing yet. Stick around, Jed, you'll be hearing from me.'

'Or about you. I don't doubt it, Saul. And I'm sorry you come to this. Mighty sorry.' And he was, I knew it, yet my hate and anger and guilt refused to let me say what was in me and I watched him go out and shut the door, leaving me to my lonely thoughts all that silent, disapproving night.

CHAPTER SIX

I SAT on the bed counting up what was left of the money I had won from Harvey in California. I thought of Harvey and of San Francisco with a rueful smile. It would be no loss if I didn't see them again. There was no sure plan in my mind, just the feeling that I'd like to see how things were in the East. I had never been there and the name of New York shone bright in the back of my mind, not yet tarnished by my experience. Maybe I could sell the gelding and buy a railroad ticket. I'd still have some dollars left for a new start and there were plenty of places I'd been, and survived, without any money in my pockets.

It was while I was thinking this way that Salena came to the door, her eyes wide and said, 'Mister Saul, Miz Bowen wants to talk with you.'

I looked up foolishly, my jaw dropping, 'What?'

The bags were lying open on my bed, I had not yet begun to pack. Behind Salena, Ilse came into view, smiling a little. Her eyes went to the bags then back to me and her smile faltered. 'Saul, may I speak with you?' Her accent was stronger with some emotion I did not recognise.

I hesitated, looking from her to Salena and Salena seemed to understand, suddenly. She started, saying, 'I'll go begin work at the Big House, ma'am.'

She went and Ilse came into my room, looking around her as she did so. I never spent much time in it, but there was a slight staleness, a lingering odour of drink and sleeplessness and sickness that shamed me, so I rose quickly and went to the window and opened it. When I turned around Ilse had shut the door and moved to my bed and sat down upon it. Her hand idly traced the collar of a shirt I had left folded upon the blanket. Without looking at me, she said, 'Were you thinking of leaving again, Saul?'

I shrugged, 'I was only visiting.'

'Where are you going?' she asked.

'East, I guess, maybe New York.'

'Why?'

'I haven't been there.' My voice held an edge of hostility.

'Do you know anyone there?'

'No. It makes no difference. I'll make out, I always do.' I paused then and met her gaze solidly, 'I don't need anyone.'

'That is sad,' said Ilse and made me angry all over again.

'And I don't need your opinion,' my voice was abrupt. 'If you came to say something, say it. I have to say goodbye to Aunt Tilda before I go.'

'Yes,' she moved, pretending she had forgotten why she had come. 'I came to ask you if you would come to live at the Big House with your father and me.'

The words did not have any meaning for me at first, then, when they had penetrated, I stood stunned and unmoving. I laughed at last, harshly. 'My God! What will Abe say to that?'

A flicker of annoyance crossed her eyes, 'He is agreeable.'

I must have lost my senses then, with nothing to say and a numbness in my brain. When I gathered them again, I stammered, 'Do you know how long it is since I set foot in that house?'

'What does it matter? Now is now and the past is over. Perhaps you and your father will at last make peace.' She shook her head. 'This is all so unnatural, this hate.' She stood up then and crossed to me and took my arm. 'Try, Saul, will you try?'

I couldn't speak. I could think of nothing, my mind in a turmoil. She said, 'Please, pack your bags. Not because you are leaving, Saul, but because you are coming home.'

Her pretty pleading confused me. I kept staring at her. 'I don't think you know what you are doing. I wish—' and I couldn't say what it was I wished.

'Abe says yes, Saul. Please come home.'

I sat down suddenly and put my head in my hands. My new found determination was gone. That hopeless longing was back and the awful need, not for drink, but the things I had lost so long ago. I had to belong again and the chance was here, waiting for me to take it. I wanted the strength to refuse but that was just foolish pride and yet the heavy feeling of doom seemed to settle around my shoulders, weighing me down with foreboding. Now, when all I wanted was offered me, and all I had to do was reach out and take it, some crazy sense of treachery, not mine, not Abe's, but life's tiptoed around me.

I said, 'Let me think,' and my voice was muffled by my hands.

The bed moved as Ilse came to sit by me. 'I'll be there. Between us, there will be peace and a proper family again. I will do my best.'

She really believed it and suddenly my shock was gone. I guess it had been shock that held me cold and fearful. Afraid, yes, for once I stepped back into that house there was nothing to stop me reliving that terrible day so long ago, and nothing to protect me from the terror and guilt and self-hatred that had haunted me. It would all come crowding back anew. Yet, if I did not, I knew I could never be free. My only chance of salvation came from facing that which had been denied me. Now, I had the opportunity. I heard my own voice, weak and faraway, say, 'It's on your own head, Ilse, you know that?'

I met her eyes and they shone with pleasure, 'Why should it be? There will only be happiness now for all of us.'

In spite of myself, I laughed a little. 'You're crazy,' but my voice was affectionate. 'I'm glad Abe married you, you know that?' And what I felt for her was warm and comforting.

Suddenly she leaned forward and kissed my cheek lightly, just in front of my ear. Though it meant little to her, it made my heart leap and there was a sudden rush of warmth in my body. She shouldn't have done that, it made things difficult again because I had a sudden dismaying fear that I could not be dispassionate with her. She was a hell of a pretty woman. 'You'll see, Saul,' she laughed, 'You come back and you'll see.' She rose, 'I'll go now and prepare your room. You tell Tilda. I know she'll be happy. Then come home to us.'

She left, going lightly, her feet eager and triumphant across the floor and out of the house. I still sat on the bed, going over it, wondering, then I shook my head and went to tell Aunt Tilda.

I should have known how happy she would be for me. She hugged me and the tears sparkled in her eyes, although she laughed. 'There, boy. It all come right for you. You come home for a purpose, this time, and everything will be all right.' She took my face in her hands and stared at me earnestly, 'Give it time and you won't be needin' that ole whisky bottle no more.'

I started. Foolishly, I thought that much of the truth about me had been spared her. Shaking my head I murmured, 'I guess you know me better than I thought you did.'

She gave an old woman's cackle. 'Every woman knows her children, natural born or not, son Saul. You didn't think you could hide from old Tilda. Even in this bed, I see what's goin' on.'

I held her close and kissed her forehead gently. 'I wish to God a good woman like you never had to be hurt, Tilda—'

'I won't be, not now. Not any more.'

I rose from the bed and picked up my bags, 'You tell Jed. You tell him I'll drop by and we can sit on the step in the evenings and talk, like always, huh?'

'I'll tell him.'

Then I left her and went out into the morning and looked at the sprawl of the Big House, trembling inside. The thought of being in close contact with Abe made my stomach turn liquid with cowardice, but I took my first steps towards the Big House and lengthened my stride with a purpose I did not feel.

As I approached, I could see the big, wide front door stood open. A dog lay across the threshold, idly snapping at passing flies. It saw me coming and rose to its feet warily, no welcome in its stiff-legged stance. It growled as I came to the foot of the porch steps and I said, 'Hey, boy,' as I mounted them. Its tail dropped and gave a small wave but it still watched me carefully. Then it gave a short warning bark as I stood in front of it. 'Be quiet, Roy!' Ilse appeared in the doorway, 'Lie down!'

The animal obeyed and she held out her hands to me. She said simply, 'Welcome home,' and her eyes shone. There was no going back for me now. Feeling a tight band clutching me by the throat, I went into the cool gloom of the house I had not entered for twenty years.

It's strange how time distorts the memory of places we remember from childhood. I don't think the place had changed, but it differed from my memory of it. The shining glory and richness I had treasured adversely as some sign of Abe's success and wealth was no longer there. It was dimmed now with the passing of years, stark in the reality of now. I looked around me. That room was still large, but smaller than I thought, the floorboards dark and highly polished. The chairs were placed as I remembered them but the tapestry of their upholstery was faded and they looked worn. The windows looked out on the sunlit pastures and they were the same, for time had not erased the truth of the house's surroundings, but inside there was a mustiness and a disappointing poorness that I had not expected.

I remembered the oil painting of the stag at bay that had always hung over the large open fireplace and I saw the animal's dainty hooves strike out over the foreign purple heather as the hounds streamed towards it. Its tongue lolled from its mouth in distress and I was struck by a chord of memory of my pity for it. Slowly, I put down my bags and stood quiet, letting the years roll back savouring days gone by, emotions and fears tumbling through me.

The bison's head hung, dusty and bleak, on the same wall; its hard glass eyes glaring blankly through the windows, out at what was left of the prairie it once had known. Abe had shot it when he first came here, before the house was built, and its flesh had sustained him and the workers for several days. I could recall him saying, not to me, to some other person, he had rarely conversed with me, that he owed his life to that animal and it would always have pride of place in the house. I lowered my eyes reluctantly, because below that buffalo's hanging, curly head Abe's terrible rifles were crossed in the usual position on their pegs. I couldn't stand the sight of them.

Beside me, Ilse was silent, watching, knowing better than to disturb my reverie. I tore my eyes from the guns and saw again the bookshelves stacked with leather-bound volumes of poetry and natural history and some novels, rescued from the remains of that other home in the South, after the war, before I was born. They had been dragged here by mule train and wagon, over the ranges and through the prairies by the people who were newly freed slaves and were now field hands and horse wranglers; workers who had elected to stay with Abe as free men but hired hands, now that the war had ended his kind of existence. I had heard that he had been a popular and fair master and had lost only half his slaves who had chosen to go to new opportunities in the North. The rest stayed with him and among them had come Tilda and her husband and their small son, Jed.

Here, in this new land in the West, they had settled and Abe had taken to doing what he loved best, raising horses and growing a few crops.

My eyes left the bookshelves and strayed over the ornaments on the mantelpiece, over my mother's ornate gold-leafed chiming clock, and my stomach began to tighten at the thought of her. Her presence was very near and I strove to push it from me. Over there, in that doorway leading to the kitchen was where it happened—I could feel a pulse high in my temple and my fists clenched at my sides. I must not think of it, could not afford to let it hurt me now. It was the heavy, glass-fronted sideboard that held Abe's store of liquor that finally held my attention. I looked at the bottles, different colours and shapes and sizes, licking my dry lips and aching in my guts.

'Is it as you remember?' Ilse's voice startled me and I jumped a little.

'I guess so,' It came out as a croak and I cleared my throat, 'Little smaller, little shabbier.'

'Things change.' Her eyes were warm with sympathy and shiny with pleasure that I was here. 'Come. Come upstairs. I have a room prepared.'

She turned and led the way towards the stairs that curved

up to the landing above. I followed the swish of her skirts, seeing the hem of her dress swirl around her black, high-heeled boots as she mounted the steps before me. It was strange hearing my heels on the wood, heavy and adult. My ears rang with the sound of smaller, racing feet, skipping down the stairway of long ago. Then we stood on the landing faced with closed doors. A sunbeam came through a small window in the wall and dust motes circled and danced in it.

Ilse opened a door. 'This is your room, Saul.'

Salena was in there, straightening a cover and she smiled across at me, welcoming. 'Hey, Mister Saul. It's good to see you here.' She faltered, embarrassed, wondering if she had said the right thing. 'I picked some flowers for you.'

Beside the bed, on a table, a vase of rapidly wilting, but still colourful prairie flowers made a bright, happy splash. I reached out and squeezed her shoulder, reassuring her. 'They're just fine, Salena. I thank you.'

She smiled, bobbed at Ilse and went out, relieved. I dropped my bags on the bed and looked around at the closet and the chest of drawers, at the washstand with the blue, flower-patterned jug of water standing in the washbowl, at the gilt-framed mirror above it. At the windows hung blue drapes and a blue home-made rug lay on the floor. 'It's good to be back, Ilse, you know that, but it'll take time, yet.' I wanted her to understand that it wasn't going to be easy. Twenty years take a hell of a lot of wiping out and it would take all of us to try, and more than that from me. I would have to be reborn. I looked at her deeply, pondering how to get it across to her. But she didn't understand, how could she? She didn't know. She was excited and flushed with success and thinking it was all going to be fine from now on. As easy as that, I thought ruefully, knowing my feelings had missed her, so I said shortly, 'Where's Abe?'

She hesitated, a small inkling of realisation showing in her eyes. The worst was yet to come. 'He is working, then he will meet a buyer in town who is interested in some of the yearlings. He will come home this evening.' She spoke faster, pushing away her sudden caution, 'But he is expecting you to be here. He will be glad to see you.'

And until that evening there was nothing for me to do but try not to let the thought of that unwanted, but inevitable, confrontation cloud my new, but shaky, hopes.

We were at supper when Abe came back. I heard his boot heels on the porch and Ilse looked up at me anxiously as I tried to disguise the sudden tremor in my hands at the sound. He came into the kitchen, still wearing his hat and he nodded to me wordlessly as he turned to hang it on a peg. I inclined my head in answer, watching him warily as he went across to Ilse and swiftly kissed her cheek. He sat down opposite me and my heart beat fast with nervousness as I tried to avoid his gaze, eating too quickly, giving myself something to do. There was no need for me to feel uncomfortable. To him, I was just an unimportant third face at the table. Ilse rose and fetched his plate and he began to eat. She said, 'Did you finish your business?'

Abe nodded, 'It went well.' He chewed in silence for a minute, master of himself and his surroundings. 'He's interested in six of the colts, wants to train racehorses and he says the two-part thoroughbreds show promise. I think he'll buy them, maybe more. He'll be here tomorrow morning.'

'I'm glad,' Ilse said.

Then Abe turned to me, 'You'll be working here, I guess?'

I swallowed, 'I'd like to.' My voice was tense and brittle.

'You'll get your keep, a few wages till I see how much you know.' Abe took another forkful of food, chewed and swallowed it and I waited. He pointed the empty fork at me, 'Jed says you're out of practice. For the time, you'll work under him and take orders from him. He knows this business as well as I do and I trust him. Whatever he says is like an order from my own mouth, you understand?'

I said, 'That suits me.'

'We'll see how you do,' Abe looked at his plate, chasing the food with his fork. 'It'll do you good, From what I hear you've been wasting your time.'

How much he knew I couldn't guess but Ilse studiously

avoided my gaze, keeping out of it. It seemed expected of me to add to what Abe had said, but I wasn't going to find excuses or try to exonerate myself. 'I've been travelling around and there wasn't much ranching in those places.'

'So I heard,' Abe's voice was dry. 'City folks don't know much about this kind of life, all they know is drinking, gambling and whoring. You'll find it hard after that.'

I cleared my throat. Maybe he knew more than Ilse and I thought he did. She was still staring down at her plate, trying to look uninvolved. Abe continued, 'But after a while, you'll find the cleanness of it all getting to you. There'll be no more city life after that.' He sat back, satisfied at his rightness.

I murmured, 'I know.'

That first week was one of the hardest I had ever faced. The need for a drink sometimes made me twist and sweat in the bed till I clenched my teeth to smother the groans that rose in my throat, but after that the urgency abated a little and it didn't hurt so much. I kept my eyes away from the liquor cabinet and I guess it could have been harder if Abe had been much of a drinker, but I never saw him touch drink while we were all together. I guess it was kept for social purposes. Maybe he and the horse buyer drank together after Abe had clinched the deal, I don't know, I had ridden out early on that second morning to find Jed and get my orders for the day. The work was hard and wasn't finished until dark so that I didn't have to spend much time in the house with Abe and Ilse. Abe didn't converse much and Ilse sewed or read in the evenings, so it was quiet and restful which suited me as I had dreaded being drawn into any kind of forced talk. What Abe's true feelings towards me were, I don't know. He showed little emotion, even towards Ilse, and none at all towards me; not pleasure, nor pain. I still felt non-existent.

Ilse continued to be pleasured by my presence, was kind and solicitous to me, and, in spite of myself, I felt gratitude towards her and once or twice a need to talk, which I had never yet allowed to intrude in my relationships. She was different, I guess, but I bit my tongue still. The time wasn't right and we were rarely alone long enough for me to give in to that sudden surprising urge.

Jed was a tough master. Sometimes it seemed that he was riding me a little too hard, picking out the worst tasks for me and hovering closely, watching, always ready to pick up a fault and blast me with it, as though I were a kid. Often I bit back a furious reply, imagining the hard black eyes of the rest of the hands resting on me with contempt. The no-good was no good. Softened by booze and women I'd never amount to anything. But I stuck it. At least, for the time being. I wanted to show them.

We had a wrangler called Dosie. He was one of the few white men among the hands. Near sixty years old he was lean and hard with a face screwed by wind and sun and open spaces. He had been on Abe's place only a few months but his reputation had preceded him and he had found work with Abe easily. He was known to be a good man with strange, new ideas, and I had never seen him work. There was a day Jed told me I'd have to learn something about horse breaking and I spent a morning watching Dosie working with the colts. The way I'd always known it, a horse was broken by breaking its spirit, by ruling it with sheer force till the exhausted animal finally gave up the unequal fight and accepted human mastery. Not so with Dosie. His voice was calm and even when he spoke to the colt, his hands gentle. We sat on the fence and watched him, some approving, silent, others with a grin of expectant triumph, waiting for him to lose out. The horse he was handling was a spunky little dun, with wide rolling eyes. He had already taught it to be led fairly quietly and it came with him into the corral amiably enough. Over one of the fence rails hung a heavy saddle and a saddle blanket, ready for the colt to learn about. Dosie led the colt to the fence rail and kept it there. Gently, with no sudden movements, he took down the blanket and showed it to the colt, talking gently all the time, then he moved to its side and placed the blanket on its back. The colt showed no panic, its ears pricked and its head against the fence rails. Dosie waited a few moments then took down the saddle and placed it across the colt's back. We watched it throw its head at the unaccustomed weight, but a few words from Dosie and it gentled again. He bent and cinched the saddle lightly but firmly then took the colt around the corral a few times, leading it by the hackamore so it could feel the strangeness of the saddle on its back and the swing of the stirrups against its flanks. After a while, Dosie said, 'That's enough,' and he led the colt back to the fence, unsaddled it and led it away to the pasture. He rejoined us with a fresh colt.

'This here,' he said, gesturing with his head to the new colt, 'has had its first lessons. He's used to his saddle and bridle. Today, he's going to be mounted.'

We sat back in satisfaction, waiting for the explosion, watching the colt accept its harness with easy good nature, hugging ourselves at the thought of Dosie's first attempt at mounting the animal. He spoke to the colt the whole time he handled it, his voice steady and gentle. The way we did it, we climbed up as quickly as we could and rode out the bucks, rears and kicks as well as we could till exhaustion overtook both man and horse. If we were thrown we got up and did it again, until the horse gave up. But I, for one, had never seen a horse this young being trained. Most cattle horses were about three years old before we even attempted to break them.

Dosie's way was different. Still talking softly, he placed a foot in the stirrups and swung up, letting the colt take his weight, then he came back to earth, patting the animal and giving it a lump of sugar as a reward. It was good-natured as a kitten. Again, Dosie swung up, and this time he came astride the colt and put his feet in the stirrups, just sitting there, letting it get to know his weight and the feel of him forking it there, its head against the fence rail, its eyes bolting a little, but no panic at all. In a little while he turned the horse's head and with slight pressure of his legs made it move and take a few steps around the corral. Then quietly, with no sudden movements, he dismounted again, patted the horse and unsaddled it.

There was no explosion of fireworks, no bucking, no frantic need to dislodge its rider. The colt was calm, friendly and unafraid. Each lesson had lasted near half an hour. Dosie turned to us. 'By the time he's three,' he said, 'He won't even know what it is to buck. Don't give them reason and they'll never learn how. Slowly and gently, with rest between lessons, we'll have the best trained, all-round-good horses in the state.'

We got down from the fence, some of the die-hards not convinced, but I felt Dosie had something and I was impressed. I said to Jed as we moved away, 'You think Dosie will let me help? I'd like to learn how he does it.'

Jed's pleasure was tangible, 'Sure,' he grinned wide, 'It's the new way and it's a damn sight better than the old. Less spoiled horses, more money for them. Abe's got sense, hiring Dosie, but he'll need to teach us how—too many horses for one man and he'll be wanting help. From now on, you be Dosie's sidekick.'

I said, 'That's fine,' really interested at last. It would be a challenge and I admired Dosie and his gentle ways.

My mood was mellow that night. For the first time, I hadn't spent the last of the afternoon worrying about Abe and his presence in the house. I was almost eager to see him so that we could talk over horse breaking methods, perhaps have a subject we could discuss together with mutual interest, and find something to share. He had been to an association meeting in town, and was late home. I was almost disappointed, waiting for him to sit with us at supper, but he was too late and we were finished by the time he arrived. Salena had gone home to Tilda, so Ilse served him his food. I heard them talking in the kitchen, so I went in to join them. Abe looked up at me, a temporary flash of irritation showing in his eyes and I felt my new found enthusiasm and resolve begin to totter a little.

Abe said, 'How come you don't ever go over and sit with Jed and his Ma in the evenings?' His impatience and resentment of my presence was concealed not at all. 'I thought you'd still be spending your time over there, mostly.'

I felt it all drain away from me, the pleasure and enthusiasm. I guessed he knew all about Dosie's methods and had watched and approved. I should have known. Whatever I had wanted to say seemed trite and contrived and pointless. Instead I said, short and abrupt, 'Sure. I had some things to discuss with Jed anyways,' and left them both quickly, but not before I noticed the trouble in Ilse's eyes.

So I went over to Jed's place and sat with them for a while. Jed was welcoming and friendly once more and Aunt Tilda and Salena were pleased for me to be with them. It was good to be there and the homely atmosphere went a little way to appease my angry disappointment.

It was late when I made my way back to the Big House, and Ilse was sitting there, reading in the lamplight, her long yellow hair loose and carefully brushed over her shoulders reflecting the glow from the light behind her. I hung my hat on a peg, avoiding her gaze. I said, 'Where's Abe?'

'Asleep. He was tired.'

Now I looked at her and saw the pity in her and was angry all over again. 'I told you it wouldn't work,' I said softly, not certain I had told her, only sure that I had told myself that.

'No, Saul. Give it time.'

I snapped, 'Time! Hell, twenty years and still give it time. For God's sakes, what's finished is finished.'

Ilse looked down at her hands, lying on the closed book. 'Please don't give up, Saul. It has been good to have you here.'

I caught the truth in her voice and something twisted in me. 'You're a good woman, Ilse. If only you knew—'

She looked up at me, her blue eyes dark and filling her face. 'Yes. It is true. If I only knew; if I could understand.'

There were a few logs almost burned out in the fireplace, and I went over to it and stirred one of the grey, ashy pieces of wood with my boot toe so that it tumbled in a shower of sparks and burst into new life.

With my back to her, I muttered, 'I guess I owe you that. Perhaps you'll give up trying when you know.'

'Then let me have the choice,' she said firmly, and when I turned and looked at her she was taut and expectant, waiting for me to speak.

So it wasn't to Abe that I opened my heart and poured it

forth, it was to Ilse and with a very different subject from the one I'd had in mind.

I hit out first with a kind of cruelty, and in a torment of guilt and self defence I said quietly, 'Abe hates me because I killed my mother.'

I heard Ilse's sharply indrawn breath of shock and horror and found, suddenly, that I could not bear to watch her face while I told her, so I turned back to the fireplace and leaned my hands on the mantelpiece and stared into the dying, flickering flames while I spoke.

'I killed her by accident, but Abe never forgave me and as far as he was concerned it could have been deliberate. I was twelve years old then.' A yellow finger of fire flickered, sprang to life, then died down as my eyes blurred with the pain of the words I had never spoken to any living soul. A few others knew, but there was no need to speak of it to them, and the subject was avoided, a shameful secret thing that never came into the open.

'I was their only child. My mother could bear no others, and Abe did not have much time for children, particularly young ones. I never remember pleasing him, playing with him or even speaking to him much. He didn't have time, building up the ranch, and no patience at all. I should have been born seventeen years old, somebody he could communicate with and mould to his way of thinking and doing things, I guess. I was afraid of him, sensing his displeasure and Ma tried to make it up to me, but it was no good because she went too far spoiling me and protecting me and worrying over me too much. More than it's good for a child who lives the rough raw way of life out here.

'So I grew uncertain, displeasing one and worrying the other and never really knowing why. My mother didn't want me to go to school with the other kids, she had been raised like a gentlewoman and she persuaded my father to have me educated by private lessons with special teachers, who came one by one and stayed a little while, then left again for various reasons.

'But I was a boy, and in spite of everything knew what was missing and that I was lacking something, so, from time to time, I behaved like a boy and was nearly always in some kind of trouble. Just for being a kid, I guess, and doing things other kids do and get away with. All I did was worry her more and make Abe more resentful at having to pay any attention to me.

'Then it was time for my twelfth birthday. I was beginning to grow up and needed things, companionship, freedom. I needed to get away from Abe's intolerance and my mother's fretting concern, though God knows, it was only her way of showing me love, and she loved me enough for both of them, her and Abe. I remember,' and I paused and stared at the dying embers, watching them blur and swim in my wet eyesight, unmindful now of Ilse, sitting quiet and tense behind me, 'I remember begging for a gun for my twelfth birthday present.

'That gun became a symbol to me. A symbol of being a person in my own right, of the need to own something that gave me power of some kind, even if it was only the power to take away the life of some jack-rabbit, or a hawk. Maybe I wanted to be good at scoring on old tin cans, so that someday someone would come to me and say, "Boy, Saul, you're good. You haven't missed a one. Every shot a bull's eye!"

'It ate into me, that need. Every day I begged her, and every day I saw the fear in her eyes and watched her shake her head. "A gun's dangerous, Saul. Don't ask. Don't ever ask. Maybe when you're grown." As for Abe, he didn't even notice. Too busy, too disinterested in me, he left my mother to deal with me, and she was too strong in her fear.

'So my twelfth birthday came, and whatever I had it wasn't a gun. I remember the hope dying in me and the wanting become stronger till I wandered through the house angry and miserable and resentful of my parents, one who didn't know me and one who couldn't trust me. I came in here,' I heard my voice break and catch in my throat, 'And looked up there,' I raised my head and stared up at the crossed rifles on the wall. Their outline shook in my sight and I felt sick but strong in the telling of this thing. 'And in a little while I dragged over a chair, climbed up on it and took one of those down.' A shudder went through me as the pictures tumbled into my mind. 'Oh, God!' I shook my head.

'I played with it a while. In those days, the guns were always loaded. I fiddled with the safety-catch and pointed the gun around the room, my finger on the trigger, making stupid kid noises, pretending to fire it, pointing it at the bison's head, at that damn' painting of a deer, out the window and when Ma came in suddenly, she screamed. I got scared. I jumped and the gun swung round at her and because my finger was still on the trigger, it tightened and the gun went off.'

My voice had dropped now, almost to a whisper. 'The bullet struck her between the eyes and there was blood in her hair and not much of her face left. I hardly knew who she was, the world was spinning, black and roaring, but there was thick warm red on her pretty dress and she was lying down, very still.

'Abe crashed in like a bull. He went crazy, I guess. I still stood there with that goddamned smoking gun and he tore it from me, nearly wrenching off my finger. "Killer!" he yelled, "You murdering little bastard killer." And he began to hit me over the head and shoulders with the gun. Though I was torn to pieces over what I had done, cold with shock and horror and fright, I still had to yell back. It was all I knew how to do. I was so sick I could only screech, "She should have let me have my own gun, she should've! She should!"

'Then everything went very quiet and while the room spun like a carousel, I heard Abe say, "I never want to see you again."

'And that was it, I guess. Aunt Tilda took me in and brought me up like her own. She always was a motherly woman, and even if I made everyone else sick to the guts, she couldn't stand to see a kid wandering around homeless and orphaned, which is what I did for a couple of days, sleeping out in the barn and scratching around for a crust to eat. I never saw Abe for a while, but I guess he knew Tilda took me in. Anyways, he didn't interfere or tell her no. What she did for me, she did on her own, giving me Jed's outgrown clothes and feeding me on what her husband and Jed earned. There was no help from Abe then, and never has been.'

CHAPTER SEVEN

AFTER I had finished speaking, I felt drained and limp. I waited for the horror in her eyes but it was gone and only sorrow and pity showed through. Ilse sat with the book on her lap, her hands still on its closed cover, looking up at me with those large eyes swimming in tears. I'd rather have the horror, I thought, I'm used to that. I can cope with it. Then the wanting hit me with physical force and I grunted, 'I need a drink after that. I guess you understand?'

I didn't care whether she did or not. I crossed to that row of shiny bottles, selected one and poured myself a long drink in one of the glasses stacked in a neat row in front of the bottles. Ilse said, 'I'm sorry, Saul. I'm so sorry.'

I drank slowly, not tossing back the drink as usual because I wanted it to last. I had to show Ilse I could stop at one because there was this crazy urge in me to prove to her I wasn't all weakness, even though I knew different.

I shrugged at her words, empty of meaning to me. 'It's over,' I said, 'Only, to Abe, it never can be. I appreciate that—but you know now why this can never work out. Every time he sees me he remembers. Every moment I'm in this house it lives with me. Look,' I pointed bitterly at the rifles on the wall, 'Why didn't he take them down? So he can torture himself forever? And me?'

She shook her head. For a moment longer I stood in front of the fire, then I put down my empty glass and turned and went upstairs, but not to sleep.

There was no change in Ilse's manner in the morning, nor in the days that followed. What I had told her, she had accepted, and if she sometimes looked at me guardedly, or sent me a sidelong, sympathetic glance, I was not aware of it. For that I was grateful. Abe was unchanged too. I guess they hadn't discussed me and as far as he was concerned Ilse knew nothing more about me than she had ever done. But he still hated me and the tension between us when he was in the house was tangible. Maybe I should have left then, listened to my inner urgings and given up. I wish to God I had, but the devil in me said stay and I listened.

Every morning, at sunup, I went with Dosie and we worked the horses, breaking them by his methods and I lost myself in the work, enjoying the challenge and feeling pride in gentling them the new way. They responded well and the horses that left us were quiet and sensible and unspoiled. The Bowen name began to grow in the horse traders' world and there was some small pride in me that I had had a hand in it, too. Jed was pleased with me, I could tell, and I spent most evenings at his place, making small talk with the hands, joshing Salena, who smiled and blushed at my teasing and sitting with Aunt Tilda, sometimes without saying anything because she was too sick most of the time. She was sinking fast and I could see the worry in Jed when he looked at her.

On Saturdays, most of the hands went into town. The whites went to the saloon and hoorawed the place, the Negroes did whatever they had to, I guess. They weren't too welcome in the saloon, and I felt sorry for the townsfolks' small minds. They didn't know they were missing out on some of the finest company. I stayed behind and they were the worst times. My guts no longer ached with a physical pain, I was over that, but my mind strayed around the things I could have been doing, and sometimes I wondered what I missed most, the wine or the women. I took to riding the boundaries by myself, on a pretence of checking fences but there wasn't much to be done. It got me out of the house and that satisfied both Abe and me.

Every Sunday, Jed drove Ilse to meeting. Abe never went and I ran out of excuses to get out of the house while Ilse was away. It got so bad that one Saturday I told her, 'Tell Jed I'll drive you to church tomorrow morning.'

Ilse smiled, 'I thank you, Saul. I don't want to be any trouble.'

I laughed a little and lied, 'Got to thinking it might do me some good. It's time I went.'

Across the room Abe glanced up sharply and I caught the gleam in his eye in the lamplight. Sardonic and humourless, his look told me all. He understood and I hadn't fooled him, but I wasn't out to play his hand. He wouldn't faze me.

I had the buggy ready for Ilse early the next morning. She looked real cool and pretty in a crisp muslin dress covered in pink rosebuds and a matching hat with a parasol dotted over in the same pink rosebuds, but they were raised from the material. I wore my best black suit and a cream stetson with a black shoestring tie hanging down the front of my shirt. I guess I wouldn't be exaggerating to say we made a handsome couple.

For Sunday-go-to-meeting, Jed used a pair of matched Morgan bays to pull the buggy, and I had risen early to prepare them. Their necks arched and they gleamed in the early sun, classy in their breeding, ready to run, and I had to hold them in firmly, they were so eager.

Ilse seemed happy and relaxed, with the breeze blowing a tendril of yellow hair against her cheek as we raced along the red-dirt trail. It felt good to be with her and it was sure good just to look at her. If only she didn't belong to Abe, if only her position didn't make her so goddam forbidding and unattainable, I might have tried to make it with her, but Abe's cloud hung over her and no matter how beautiful she was this morning the vision of his face, and that other one, hung between us, visible only to me. She was unaware of anything but the fine, bright summer morning and the feel of going somewhere to do her good soul more good.

The meeting house rose before us on the outskirts of town, whitewashed and clean, gleaming in the bright sun. Folks streamed from all directions, dressed in their best, chattering like magpies, some on foot, others in buggies, and children ran in and out of the throng, doing things kids do, furtively pinching here and there, dropping into innocence when suspicious eyes turned their way. It was a good feeling and a happy sight. A bell tolled sonorously and I almost belonged—for a moment, only.

I pulled in the Morgans and hitched them to a tree in the

shade, to wait for us, then I turned to help Ilse down. Someone called 'Mornin', Miz Bowen!' and she looked up and smiled happily then I saw her expression falter a little. My eyes followed hers to the matron who had greeted her. She was a big woman with a small, straggly-moustached husband and three or four shiny-scrubbed kids. But her eyes were on me and they were hostile and unwelcoming. Normally I wouldn't have given a damn, but this morning it rankled and, deliberately, I tipped my hat to her and her husband. They ignored me, their eyes swivelled away and they turned their backs.

Several times, on the path to the church, folks started to greet Ilse and their words caught in their throats as they recognised me and they choked in outrage and righteous indignation. In spite of myself, I felt my cheeks burn with anger though I guess I shouldn't have expected anything else.

Inside the church, with the sun streaming through the pale colours of the stained-glass windows (brought all the way from New York, they said), silence fell on the fidgeting, whispering congregation as we passed each half-filled pew and I heard the whispering start up again behind our backs, with renewed vigour. Two high spots of colour showed on Ilse's cheeks when I glanced at her sideways and I was suddenly ashamed that my company should have inflicted this pain upon her. We took our places and I sat on the hard wooden bench, burningly aware of the tension around us and I took up the hymn book before me, leafing through the pages and sightlessly scanning the words dancing in front of my eyes, trying not to notice Ilse's bowed head and folded hands.

I don't remember much of that service, the first in years and the last I ever attended. The Reverend droned his prayers and chanted his hymns in a toneless, bored voice but he sure came to life in his sermon. He was yelling fire and brimstone and there were choruses of 'Amens' and 'Hallelujahs' fit to frighten all the devils for miles. It was when he went on to the evils of drinking and gambling and whoring that I became tighter and tenser than ever. He didn't mention me by name, but he might as well have done. The old sinner never took his eyes from my face and I felt the attention of the whole congregation was turned in my direction, whether it really was or not. He was all but frothing at the mouth as he roared 'Woe' and 'Damnation' and 'Eternal fires' for those who could not repel Satan and his bodily lusts, and the end for those who had killed in passion was beyond even his eloquent turn of phrase.

The sermon must have lasted all of half an hour and ended on a rising, jubilant, triumphant wail of 'Amen!' from the folks around us. I guess he would have kept going, but by then the Reverend was red and sweating and out of breath and it flashed through my mind that he looked like a man in need of a drink, so he finished, and soon afterwards so did the service. I sat bolt upright the whole time, meeting his righteous gaze, trying to hide the turmoil inside me, not for my sake but for Ilse who sat with her head bowed and her eyes cast down at the nervously twitching hands in her lap.

I heard the sound of the congregation rising and starting to go out, so I rose and offered Ilse my arm. She started, when I moved, as though she had been lost in thought somewhere far from here. I guess that's where she wanted to be. Then she rose, too, and took my arm with her little hand, laying it soft as a dove on the cloth of my coat. I saw her chin come up and in her flushed pink face her bright eyes flashed blue sparks of defiant pride. Slowly and deliberately, she looked straight into my eyes and her pretty mouth lifted in a smile of fondness and kindness that all but stopped my heart. Suddenly, we were alone in that crowd of milling, disapproving people. There was a glow around her that dimmed everything that had gone before and it hit me in the pit of my stomach with a strength that took away my breath.

Together, heads high, we made our way back down the aisle to the entrance where the Reverend was greeting his flock. Faces were a blur to me, but one I recognised with a small surprise. In the dimness at the back of the church, dressed in an unseemly red was the girl I had seen in the saloon. For a moment I struggled to remember her name and then it wormed into my mind. Abbie, that was it. Beside her was her man, Tolley, the one I had fought with. His face was grim and his eyes hard on mine, but I ignored him and looked instead at Abbie. I guess even bar girls need to pretend respectability and she was nowhere near as bad as I was, so I had no right to feel shock at her presence. If she was astonished at mine, she did not show it. Instead there was a friendly warmth in her eyes and she smiled at me, unashamedly. She was the only one who did, so I touched my hand to my hat brim and bowed my head slightly as I passed her, feeling a little sadistic pleasure in Tolley's sudden flush of anger.

Ilse hadn't noticed either of them, struggling as she was with the humiliation I had brought on her. At the door, the Reverend shook hands with those who passed through and then it was our turn. He turned to Ilse his smile bright and false. 'A pleasure to see you, Mrs Bowen. I trust you are well?' He held out his hand to Ilse and she took it, a little limply, I felt.

'Quite well, Reverend Taylor.' Then she shocked us both, 'May I introduce my stepson, Saul Bowen, who has been in San Francisco for some years.'

We neither of us wanted the confrontation, but he had to play the part of a man of God. Turn no man away—knock and it shall be opened to you, even Saul Bowen, I guess, so he held out his hand flaccidly and showed his teeth and said faintly, 'Yes. I had heard you were home, Mister Bowen.'

Some devil in me made me grasp his dead-fish fingers with a painful firmness. I drowned his gasp with a loud, 'I had figured that, Reverend. Mighty powerful sermon—mighty powerful!'

His eyes turned stony, 'If it helps, Mister Bowen, if it helps then I will have done my duty.'

'You sure try, Reverend.' I touched my hat brim and led Ilse away.

We were alone this time. The congregation parted to let us through, clearing a path for us as though we would somehow contaminate them with any contact and no one called a greeting now. Silently, I handed Ilse into the buggy, unhitched the Morgans and drove away. We were silent most of the way home. I couldn't bring myself to apologise to Ilse for being the means of bringing shame upon her so I said nothing but seethed inwardly at what had happened. What I was was no fault of hers and I despised those so-called Christians who made her suffer for being what they should have been.

It was Ilse who broke the silence. 'I will never go there again, they are bad people.'

I didn't want her to feel that way. Sunday meetings had been a thing of pleasure for her and a source of comfort. It made things worse that she should be denied that because of me. 'Sure you will—' I said, tautly, 'but Jed will drive you.' She clucked her tongue impatiently, but I paid no heed. Deep inside, I seethed with the need to show the whole uncharitable lot of bastards just what evil I could bring on them, and by God, I would.

I set out to prove it the next Saturday. Still churning with anger and vengeance, I dressed in my best again that evening. I looked one hell of a dandy. For a passing moment, I toyed with the idea of taking my gun with me. I was primed for trouble wasn't I? But there was something, a kind of constriction in my stomach, a tight hold around my throat that held me back. I even went to my bags to look at the gun nestling down there at the bottom, under my belongings. It gleamed dully in the darkness, almost pulsating with a strange life of its own and I knew if I touched it just once, here in my mother's unseen presence, I was finished. It was superstition I guess, and cowardice, but I never made any claims to being a brave man. If I had been anywhere else but here, if I was going to any other town but that one, it would have made no never mind to me, but the past bound me with links stronger than those the sheriff could throw on me, and feeling slightly sick and shaken, I closed the bag again. I'd take my chances unarmed. I knew I was crazy.

Then I went to fetch the gelding. I bumped into Jed in the corral and he looked at me a little nervously, I felt. 'Going to town, Saul?'

I glared at him defiantly, 'By hell, I am. Man needs a little break once in a while.'

He said, trying to hide the trouble in his mind, 'Take care of yourself.'

'I don't need no nursemaid. You should accept that, Jed.'

He shrugged, 'Sho' nuff,' the southernness drawling out of his voice in a careless, easy way but I knew he was shook up. Even so, I knew that if he tried to stop me or suggested going with me I'd have to point out that my guardian angel wasn't some black horse wrangler. By God, even if I had to prove it by a little violence to his handsome African face.

I pushed the gelding hard on my way to town and it lathered badly when we were only half-way there, so I slowed it to a walk and had a little time to think. I was a mite shocked by my thoughts on Jed. I had never considered him racially before, and I didn't like my new attitude. He was my brother in all but blood, and my wellbeing was as important to him as it was to me, I knew that. I put it down to the broiling hate in me and shrugged it away. Tonight, I'd show them and tomorrow I'd be full of brotherly love for Jed again. First there was now and what I needed to do.

CHAPTER EIGHT

It was a typical Saturday night in a western town. I could hear the revellers while I was still a half mile away and could see the glow in the sky from the town lights. A big yellow moon hung in the heavens and the gelding and I were two impatient black shadows on the trail.

We entered Main Street and I headed for the saloon. There were plenty of horses tethered to the hitch-rail and I guessed it was a full-to-busting place and I started itching for a little of the action I had missed for so long. Inside, it was bright and gay with colour and stank of liquor fumes, sweat and cheap perfume. Bar girls moved among the throng like washed-out butterflies, their screeches of laughter shrill and false, and someone played a tinny piano badly. Shouldering my way to the bar, I saw faces I knew and some I thought I recognised. Some of the ranch hands were there and they acknowledged me with nods or half-raised hands but they didn't seem to want to get involved or come over so I dismissed them as of no importance. I didn't need company to get good and drunk—I was used to doing it on my own.

It was the same bartender who had been there the last time. I'd brought trouble to the place and I could see from the look in his eyes when he saw me that I wasn't too welcome, and it only served to make me madder. He didn't want to serve me and left me standing there longer than was necessary, so I banged my fist on the bar top and yelled some, so pretty soon he came up to me. I paid for a shot of rye and drank it in one gulp and ordered another, neat. He gave it to me, avoiding my eyes, and I noticed there was a little space around me so that I was alone in the crowd. Hell, even those bad-time boozers thought they were better than me and I began to get really riled.

I had a couple more drinks, and the old feelings were back. I was calming down and the only important thing was the fine taste of that whisky and the good things it was doing to my belly and brain. It was just about the most important thing in the world and made life worth living. Then I called for the bottle, not caring at last, knowing soon that there'd be nothing for me but that piss-coloured liquid until the sweet darkness came and took us both away.

The bottle came sliding across the bar towards me and I reached for it eagerly and began to pour a little into my glass. Someone put a hand on my arm and I glanced down in irritation at having been interrupted. 'It's Mister Bowen, ain't it, honey?'

It was that Abbie girl and she was standing there shaking my arm a little, her eyes all bright and shiny and her red hair piled high on her head. She wore a green velvet gown that set off her pale skin and bright hair so well that in that smoke-filled, noisy room it was hard for me to make out the lines of hard use on her face.

I said, good-humouredly enough, 'That's me, Saul Bowen, devil.'

She giggled, 'Oh, now, I've heard things about you and I don't believe a one of them, I saw you myself in church on Sunday. No devilry in that!'

I looked down at her, keeping the mockery from my voice, 'They say the devil turns up in the strangest places. I saw you too.'

'My name's Abbie.' She had lowered her voice to a false huskiness and I knew what she was after, but I sensed, underneath, there was a certain excitement in her. 'Maybe this time you'll buy me a drink?'

'I'd like that fine, but I notice you're spoken for. Where's your feller?'

'You mean Tolley?' She grimaced a little, 'He thinks he can tell me what to do. He'll learn, some day. I don't belong to no one!'

'Well, that's good to know. Wouldn't like to think I was wasting my time.' I heard the flippant words fall from my mouth and thought hell, I didn't even want her, but she was better than nothing and showed willing. Maybe I should take advantage of that. She was the only one who was even half-way friendly.

I called for a drink for Abbie and saw her receive a warning look from the barkeep, but she chose to ignore it. We made our way to an empty table in a dim corner and we sat there and toasted each other with our eyes, silently holding up the glasses before drinking. I had stumbled on the way to the table and Abbie put a guiding arm around my waist, thinking I was drunk already, but I had a long ways to go yet. Still, the uncertainty in my legs should have warned me that I was a little out of practice.

I took three drinks to Abbie's one and the noise around us was getting kind of indistinct. The piano player was still thumping the keys and someone sang 'I dream of Jeannie' off key. God knows what tune the piano player was thinking of. They were both at odds with one another. Abbie talked to me some, but I wasn't really listening, I was watching her as I got drunker and thinking she wasn't so bad after all. In fact, the warmth in my stomach was giving way to a greater heat that wasn't caused by the whisky. Abbie was prattling away at me and I said, cutting off her sentence, whatever it was, 'You got a room upstairs?'

She stopped for a moment, mouth open, then, surprisingly, flushed, 'Well, yes, I guess there's one—'

'What are we waiting for? We can finish this up there.' I took the almost empty whisky bottle by the neck.

She hesitated, something indefinable in her eyes, almost a nervousness.

'You think I can't pay?' I almost snarled. 'You think I'll waste your time? I ain't that drunk.' I reached forward and took her hand in mine, 'Or do you think the devil's got ways a respectable whore can't handle?'

Again that flicker of excitement and she lost her nervousness. 'You ain't no devil, Saul Bowen.' Her fingers stirred in mine, setting my blood tingling, 'I'll prove to you I ain't no angel either.' Her voice had turned husky and low and suddenly I couldn't wait, so I gripped her arm and brought her to her feet and rose with her. 'Let's go,' I said.

We pushed through the crowd and I knew everyone was looking at us, wary, as we made our way through to the dimly lit stairs that led to a wooden balustraded landing. We were on about the fourth stair up when there was a roaring behind us that drowned even the strains of 'Jeannie' and something gripped the back of my collar with a clutch of iron. I heard a whoop as I slid backwards down the stairs and landed heavily on the wooden sawdust-covered floorboards, my precious whisky bottle flying from my hand. I lay on my back, winded, looking up into the red enraged face of Tolley. He was still roaring.

Too late, I saw the kick coming and tried to avoid it but it landed in my ribs with a force that crushed me and drove the air from my lungs, leaving me doubled in agony. Tolley tried again, aiming at my groin but I wasn't going to give him that pleasure. Befuddled though I was, I was quick enough to grab his boot with both hands and I lifted it upwards and twisted it at the same time. He yelled as he landed beside me on the floor and I rolled and threw myself at him, landing astride him.

'What the hell's got into you?' I shouted, plunging my hands into his hair and raising his head towards me. He tried to heave his body to rid himself of me and I began to beat the back of his head on the floor with solid, brain-jarring thuds that made his eyes roll and his teeth rattle audibly. 'You owe me a goddam half bottle of whisky,' I gritted between clenched teeth.

From nowhere, the heel of his hand came up and caught me on the point of the chin then across my adam's apple with a force that lifted me clear off his prone body. I was dimly aware of a spiteful burst of cheering and knew, without a doubt, that the crowd wasn't on my side. Now I had to show them, more than ever. There was a forest of legs around us and Tolley was struggling to his feet in the circle they had cleared for us. The barman was shouting worriedly, but we paid him no mind. I guess he was concerned for his furnishings and his big mirror and who'd pay for the damages.

Tolley came for me again, keeping his half crouch, swinging wildly. If I'd been half-way sober, I could have taken him and finished it neatly, but I was slow and clumsy with drink so that he was on me again before I could collect myself. He was an ugly, unprofessional attacker, all bluff and bluster and ungainly wide blows that would have served him no good against a sober, habitual fighter. Me, I was so unsteady that his bull-like rushes had me down every time and his fists connected too often. I could feel my face swelling and my lips split so I tasted blood.

The sight of it made the crowd roar again and I shook my head to clear my eyes of sweat. One of my punches got home and Tolley staggered back against the bar so that his flailing arms cleared it of bottles and glasses and they flew every which way, smashing against walls and tumbling to the floor, sending shards of glass and splashes of liquor high in the air so that those nearest ducked to avoid being hit, crunching their boot heels on the splinters on the floor.

Tolley came rushing back at me, his eyes wild and his mouth flecked with spittle. 'You bastard,' he gasped, 'Abbie's my girl!' And that's when we all stopped still. He held a gun in his hand. I hadn't seen him draw it and the breath went out of me. Dimly, I knew the onlookers had drawn well back and in the recesses of the saloon there was a movement and the sudden rush of fresh air and the creak of the batwing doors as some let themselves out and went away. No one wanted to stop a bullet, most of all me.

Then Abbie said, still standing on that fourth stair, 'God-sakes, Tolley, I tol' you I ain't your girl. I ain't no one's girl!'

I didn't take my eyes from Tolley's gun but I felt a flash of gratitude and admiration for her. She had guts because I was sure as hell unpopular and she was siding with me against them all. I don't know why it is, but there's always a woman will do that; stay with a man against them all, even though she knows he's no good. Maybe there's some kind of attraction in laying with the mad dog, some kind of crazy excitement. Whatever it was, Abbie was taking Tolley's attention.

Only for a moment he looked at her, his lips drawing back from his teeth and that was when I rushed him. I didn't fancy having that gun pointing at me a moment longer, so I closed in and by the time he realised it, I had his arm in both my hands and the gun was pointed high and away. There was a movement of his trigger finger and I heard a shot blast past my cheek and the shattering of that big mirror behind the bar.

Now most dived for cover, behind chairs and upturned tables and behind the piano. I saw the barkeep duck down behind the counter even though pieces of that long mirror kept breaking away and falling down all around him. Tolley and I still struggled for the gun, his breath coming short and fast, smelling of stale tobacco and something he had eaten, filling my nostrils and turning my guts. I guess the stale whisky I gave back was no easier to stomach. He was swearing low, and no one else made a sound, except I grunted a little with the exertion. Abbie watched from her place on the stairs, wide-eyed and pale and speechless.

We were belly to belly and chest to chest, Tolley and I, and I kept his gun hand up in the air with the strength of desperation. Against my legs I felt his own striving for purchase and then he stepped on that whisky bottle of mine, one of the few that remained unbroken in that place. His foot went sideways and I heard the empty bottle roll and spin and for an instant he was off balance, his grip relaxed. I reached quickly, twisted and the gun was in my hand now, pointing at his stomach. He paused, his mouth wide and panting, his eyes burning up with hate and he spat, 'You no-good mother-killer!' and jumped at me. The words shrieked through my brain, echoing like the dying wail of some tormented lost soul and before they died away my finger had tightened involuntarily on the trigger. The gun bucked in my fist, but I didn't hear the blast. I could only hear his last words though I saw him clearly enough. He grasped his stomach and bent forward, his eyes rolling up in his head till the balls were out of sight and I saw the gush of blood spurt between his fingers and tumble down his legs. He fell forward in a crouch, ass in the air, head turned sideways along the reddened, sawdust-covered floor and the gun fell from my fingers beside him. Now there was a noise again; a great exhalation of breath and a sudden concerted movement towards us.

I just stood there, stunned and sickened and wanting to run, but I couldn't move. No one touched me or looked at me. They were clustered around Tolley and I couldn't see him any longer. It was then Abbie came back down the stairs and joined them. I heard her speaking and someone answered her and she came to me. People were moving around now with urgency. She said, 'Tolley's alive. They've sent for the doctor.' She put a hand on my arm and faced them all, 'You saw that,' she raised her voice, 'Saul Bowen wasn't even armed, you saw that! It was a fair fight and you all know Tolley started it. If anyone wants to see Saul, he'll be at my place. He ain't runnin' anywhere 'cause there ain't no reason for him to run. You tell Sheriff Byrnes that.'

She pulled at me and I went with her, out of that smoke-filled, gunpowder-smelling, boozy place into the cool night air. I hardly knew where I was going. Abbie helped me along and I staggered beside her not really aware of anything but those last frightful moments in the saloon. They played themselves over and over in my mind and though Abbie spoke to me I didn't hear a word she said. Somehow we reached her place, a tumbledown shack on the outskirts of town. It didn't look too bad in the moonlight though I guessed it was mighty shabby when the sun shone on it. We walked all the way and I never gave the gelding a thought, tethered patiently at the hitch-rail at the saloon, I was so numb and stupefied. As we went up the path to the shabby front door, even in the moonlight I could see the paint hung from it in strips, thin and brittle. Abbie kept crooning, 'Weren't your fault, honey, don't take on so.' I did understand that.

I stood stupidly inside as Abbie left me and watched her in the moonlight streaming through the window as she went to light the oil lamp. The room lit with a dull yellow glow as she replaced the smoke-grimed glass chimney and drew together a pair of short, moth-eaten drapes. I looked around me with no great interest. There was only one room with a couple of wooden chairs, a scrubbed wooden table, a closet and a bed in one corner. The bed was mighty fancy, big and gleaming with brass and covered with a chintz spread patterned with twining roses. Somehow, it made the rest of the place look poorer and shabbier, but I guess the bed was the most important part of it. It flashed wryly through my mind that it had to be, it was her living.

Abbie stepped up to me, her eyes huge and shadowy in the dim lamplight and she raised a hand and touched my split lip with a gentle finger-tip. I winced a little and she said, 'There's water in the yard, I got me a well there. If you want to wash up you'll have to do it outside. Ain't no neighbours to see.' She smiled and I saw her teeth flash, white and even, 'Never could find anyone wanted to live near me.' There was no regret in her, just simple acceptance and a pleasing honesty. I thought she was quite a girl and suddenly I was lonelier than ever.

I said roughly, 'Not now, Abbie—' and put my hands on her waist and she came to me willingly, reaching up for my mouth and finding it, cut and bruised though it was. Her warmth and need was too much for me. I felt the tears rise in my throat and I kissed her almost brutally, trying to find in her the answer to what I was and what I wanted. It wasn't there, but in the meantime she sufficed and gave me comfort.

In the lamplight, she reached up and unpinned her hair and it fell in glowing masses about her shoulders, then she turned her back to me and said, thickly, 'Unfasten my dress,' standing with her head bowed while I fumbled clumsily with all those damn buttons, and then there were the hooks on her corset. Her clothes fell about her feet and lay like ruins and then she turned to face me, pale and naked and raised her arms above her head like a picture of some goddess I saw somewhere, rising from the sea. But Abbie wasn't a goddess, just a whore who knew her job and had a soft place in her heart for loners and freaks.

The bed was wide and soft and dragged me down into its depths with Abbie beside me and under me and over me all night long and while I took her I kept remembering all I was and all I had been and all I had done and couldn't understand what it was she found to want in me.

CHAPTER NINE

SHERIFF BYRNES came to Abbie's shack soon after first light. I was still asleep and the sound of voices awakened me. I struggled into consciousness and was pulling on my pants when I heard his horse moving away. Abbie came in, fully dressed. She must have been up for some time.

'That was the sheriff,' she said.

'I heard. Is he coming back?'

'No. Not for you.'

'Well, I'm surprised!' I turned to pick up my shirt. 'What stopped him? I thought sure he'd be wanting me.'

'Oh, he wants you alright. Ain't a thing he can do about it.' She was smiling.

I fumbled with my sleepy astonishment, relieved that I was still free. 'There's enough townsfolk would like to see me back in his jail,' I said. 'Don't tell me they've turned noble?'

'Oh no, Tolley did.'

'Tolley?' My mouth gaped open.

'He'll live. He lost a lot of blood but that bullet didn't touch none of his vitals. He told the sheriff it was his fault and felt no blame for you.'

'Why? Why Tolley?'

She laughed now, 'Tolley's a fool but he's crazy about me. He's too scared to do anything might rile me and turn me off him so he figured he'd pleasure me by not letting any harm come to you.' She lowered her voice and came to me, starting to fasten my shirt buttons. 'He was right,' she murmured and reached up to kiss me.

'Oh my,' I grinned now, 'I guess that's going to make some folks mighty mad!'

'As hornets.' She gave a little giggle.

She fixed eggs and coffee for breakfast on the little black stove in the corner of her shack. Tendrils of grey smoke came from the joints in the stovepipe and the room smelled of it and the frying eggs and the strong coffee. It was shabby but cosy in spite of needing fixing. I liked it.

I rose, having eaten my fill. My head was pounding with a sudden aching, a legacy of the night before. 'I'll be moving on,' I said. 'I recollect I left a good horse outside the saloon.'

She busied herself collecting the plates. 'You'll be back?' She did not look at me.

'Soon.' And I meant it.

Outside, the air was fine and clear, with a hint of warmth to come later. The town seemed very quiet until I remembered that this was Sunday morning. All those stomping hell-raisers would be in the church, I guessed, listening to the Reverend preaching his hell fire. The saloon was shut and deserted and there was no one on the boardwalk, though I noticed a few window curtains fluttered as I passed. That poor old gelding was still saddled up at the hitch-rail, his head drooping in boredom, feeling neglected. He even pricked up his ears and gave a few grunts of welcome when he saw me and I was quite flattered that he cared. He was hungry and thirsty, I guess, and hoped I'd see to his needs at last.

I untethered him and led him to the water-trough, loosening the girth a little so that he could drink. He lowered his head and sucked greedily and I stood beside him, rolling a smoke while I waited. There was the sound of wheels in the street and I looked up quickly to see Jed driving towards me in the buggy. Goddam, he'd likely brought Ilse in to church and here I was frayed and used, maybe with the marks of last night's fight still plain on my face. I felt a quick irritation at his presence.

He pulled in the horses beside me and stared down at me searchingly, 'You all right?' He seemed always to be asking that.

I said shortly, 'Of course. Why not?'

'I heard talk.'

The gelding was finished so I turned to cinch him again, 'Nothing to worry about,' I said. Mounting, I rode to Jed. 'You bring Miz Bowen in?'

He shook his head and started the horses, falling into step

beside me. 'Not this morning. She's resting. She was up all night at my place tending to Ma.'

'Aunt Tilda?' I glanced at him sharply.

'She took a real bad turn. Thought sure we was going to lose her. Miz Bowen saw the lights was on and came down from the Big House and stayed with her, helping Salena and me.' He grinned, a flash of white in the darkness of his face. 'I think she thought maybe you was giving trouble.'

'Go to hell, Jed,' I said.

He sobered again, 'That's a real good woman, Saul.'

'I know.'

'Ma was calling for you.'

'I'm sorry. I didn't know that.'

'Yeah. 'Tweren't your fault. Half-way through the night we got a message from some of the hands you was in trouble in the saloon. Shot a man.' And his eyes on me were as hard as marbles.

'He'll live. He started it, so I'm in the clear.'

'Yeah? It sure upset Miz Bowen.'

'Hell! Did you have to tell her?' Anger and guilt coloured my voice.

'She was right there when Sam was tellin' us. Couldn't help but hear. That's why she sent me in this morning. See if I could find out what was going on.'

I said nervously, 'Abe?'

'He don't know a thing. Leastways, I don't think so. No telling what he'll hear though.'

'Goddam,' I said and felt like turning around and riding back to Abbie. But we kept going, up the trail towards home.

I went straight to Aunt Tilda when we got back. She looked tiny and wasted in that big bed. I felt there was nothing left of her but her fighting spirit and that was fierce and alive in her eyes. She held out two thin, clawlike hands to me and I grasped them with a sort of desperate need to show her how much I cared. 'You caused some trouble last night. Don't you go doin' that again,' I said to her.

Her laugh was breathless and weak. 'Son Saul, it was only to get your attention.'

'You've always got that.' I patted her hands, 'So no more actin' up.'

'You're a good boy, Saul. A good boy—' Her eyes closed and she fell asleep at once, exhausted. I drew away from her, feeling bad. I sensed the end was very near.

I crept around at the Big House, avoiding Abe successfully, hoping I wouldn't have to face Ilse just yet. She must have been still asleep because I didn't see her till later in the afternoon. I had been on my bed in my room, smoking cigarette after cigarette. The mirror had shown me there were marks on my face and my lips were puffy and swollen from Tolley's knuckles, but it could have been worse. I heard Ilse coming and she knocked on my door. When I opened it, her face was showing her anxiety, her blue eyes wide and troubled. She slipped in quickly, closing the door behind her, her gaze searching me with concern.

'Jed said you managed to get away with it this time.' She came straight to the point, I had to give her that.

'Maybe you don't know the whole story.' I turned away embarrassed by the way she stared at my bruises. 'It wasn't my doing.'

'You mean you weren't drunk?' There was a little sharpness in her and I flushed. She wasn't my mother, no matter how much she wanted to be, and even if she had been, I wouldn't have taken any fussing from her.

'I had a few drinks.' I threw defiance and not contrition at her, 'But that's my affair. The ruckus was over a girl, not booze.'

'A girl?' There was a sudden hesitation and a small shadow passed over her eyes, quickly masked. I wondered over that, for a moment.

'A real nice girl. Name's Abbie. I'll be seeing her again.'

Now Ilse smiled fleetingly. 'Saul, I'm glad. Perhaps that's what you need. Someone you can care for and take pride in.'

Here she was, matchmaking—her husband's son and a whore! Poor Ilse, I guess she would have been shocked if she had known. I almost told her, I wanted to shock her because she was once again so all-fired holy and innocent and goddam noble. And too lovely to be in my room alone with me, with the door closed and no one to see what happened between us. The realisation hit me suddenly and I gulped trying to push away the wanting in me. I suddenly needed to take Ilse in my arms and feel those sweet lips against mine. I wondered if she would push me away in disgust and loathing, but later she would give in—I knew she would, if I took the first step—possibly something showed in me. We had been silent a moment, looking at each other and I noticed a little warm colour rise in Ilse's cheeks. She spoke quickly, 'Then you must bring her here, Saul. Abe and I will want to meet her. Bring her to dinner one evening, soon. Yes, Abe will be glad to meet her.'

She was bringing Abe between us like a barrier, a certain guard against what I was planning for her. Whether it was deliberate, I don't know, but it sure worked.

'I'll do that,' I said harshly, picturing Abbie in her painted whore's face and cheap perfume sitting opposite Abe and Ilse at dinner. It pleased me. I might just do that, for the pleasure of Ilse's reaction. I'd shake her yet, because sure as hell, my drinking and fighting didn't seem to faze her.

At dinner that night, Ilse told Abe, 'Saul has a girl. I said he must bring her to meet us.'

Abe grunted, hardly looking up. 'I guess she has a kick like a mule judging from your face, boy.'

I swallowed, knowing my vain hope that the candlelight would disguise my bruises had failed. I said, 'Just a little high spirits left over from last night.' What the hell, so he'd be likely to find out anyways.

'Just keep them "high spirits" away from here, you remember that.' His eyes met mine with malice and I froze with hate. He saw it too. 'You're here because my wife felt it would help you. I don't see any change yet, and as far as I can figure you're still an ungrateful son of a bitch. I'm giving you a warning, Saul. You repay this lady here the way she wants you to or you can go and get yourself lost in damnation for ever. It makes no never mind to me. Never did.'

That was enough for me. I saw Ilse's stricken face and

Abe's hard one as I rose quickly and left the table and went out. I sure as hell wasn't going to take any of Abe's drink, but I needed one badly, more then ever, so that it wrenched at my guts and made me sick to my stomach. I didn't feel like going over to Jed's place; Aunt Tilda's deathbed wasn't where I wanted to be, even though I knew I owed her so much. So, I saddled the gelding and rode to Abbie's shack, stopping at the saloon to get a bottle of whisky on the way. It wasn't too crowded and I got my share of cold, hard stares, but I wasn't staying anyways.

Abbie was glad to see me and we shared the bottle of whisky and got drunk together in her bed. It helped me forget a little.

CHAPTER TEN

I HUNG around with Abbie for a couple of days, trying to get the miseries out of my system. She knew I was tensed up and ready for a fight but not the reason for it. I left her not knowing, saddled the gelding and headed back for the ranch, not sure if I was going to stay or collect my things. Something in me wanted to see Ilse once more and the pull was too strong to ignore, even though I was sure I would have to face up to Abe again. I guessed I'd be yellow and high-tail it away from there as usual, though my hate for him was tangible, hammering at my brain and in my guts and there was a desire at the back of my mind, a need to hurt him and hurt him bad.

But I forgot all that when I got back. I knew there was something wrong as I rode through the gateway. The hands were clustered around Jed's place and there were a couple of buggies I didn't recognise standing in the shade of the apple tree beside the shack. I didn't go on to the Big House but let the gelding go loose in the corral and made my way over to Jed's. Some of the men glanced at me sideways as I pushed through them and I noticed they were cleaned up and dressed in their best, wearing their hats and solemn expressions. When they spoke to each other their voices were low, almost whispers, and no one spoke to me.

I went up on the porch, my boot heels making a loud clatter on the boards and I was aware of my rumpled clothes and unshaven cheeks, but I didn't know why it should have mattered. I soon found out. Inside Jed's living-room was a group of people I didn't know and with them were Jed and Salena and Ilse. They all looked up at me as I stepped inside and stood there gazing at them. Ilse looked pale and tired and Salena's eyes were red from crying. Jed seemed suddenly old and drawn, his face hard and his mouth tight with held-in grief.

Ilse said, 'Saul—' and her eyes were troubled.

Jed finished for her, 'Ma's dead.' He showed no softening in his tone. It was a flat, cold statement for me and, though I had expected it, the blow was just as bitter and cruel as he meant it to be.

I felt my face go pale with shock and the sorrow of it. My hat felt heavy on my head and I snatched it off and felt the tears prick my eyes. My voice, when I found it, was harsh and cracked. 'When did it happen?'

'Sunday night.' Jed watched me closely.

'She's been gone two days? Why didn't anyone tell me?'

'There's been plenty to do without runnin' around lookin' for you,' Jed said coldly. 'We just about to bury her. This here's the minister,' He indicated a tall black man in black clothes, clutching a Bible to his chest who looked at me with eyes of jet stone. 'And this here's the undertaker.' He indicated another.

I nodded at them wordlessly, the room beginning to spin a little around me. 'Coffin's in the bedroom,' Jed said tightly, 'Sealed up now, so you can't see her, but you can go look if you want to.'

I moved my head again, 'Yeah,' I husked, 'yeah, I want to look.'

Jed turned towards Aunt Tilda's bedroom and I followed him in. He shut the door behind us and we were alone in that room so full, still, of her presence. The sun came through the windows and dusty beams played on the dark wood of the brass-handled coffin that rested on the empty, bare bed. I said brokenly, 'Aunt Tilda—' twisting my hat brim in my hands.

'She wanted you, Saul. Lord, how she called for you! Sent someone lookin' but there was no knowin' where you was. Heard tell you was in the saloon buyin' whisky and that was all. I guessed if you got a skinful you could have been anywhere, and if we did find you, you wouldn't be good for nothin'. You surely wouldn't have been any comfort to Ma, not in the state you get into.'

The dislike in Jed's voice crawled under my skin and set my stomach churning with added guilt. I stammered, staring at that shiny, polished coffin, 'I was with a girl, name's Abbie. She's got a shack just outside of town.'

'Don't matter. Don't matter now. We got us a buryin' to do. You comin' to that?'

'For God's sake, Jed, you think I'd have had this happen?' Maybe my raised voice was all wrong in that room. It must have been heard by the mourners outside. 'You think it doesn't tear me up inside to know she's gone? She was as good a mother to me as she was to you. There's nothing left for me now Tilda's gone.'

For a moment there was a softening in him and he said, more gently, 'Well, let's go bury her and give her the kind of funeral a saint like her deserves. She'll be glad you're here now.'

When we went out, Abe was there with Ilse. He didn't speak to me and hardly glanced my way. He shook Jed's hand and patted Salena's shoulder while she burst into sudden sobs. Jed said to me, 'You'll take one of the handles?' I nodded and we went back into the bedroom.

Jed and I stood at the head of the coffin and two of the hands positioned themselves behind. Together we lifted the heavy casket and carried it through the living-room on to the porch and into the sunlight. Abe's good buggy stood there with the Morgans in the traces, held still by a coloured hand. They arched their necks and their rich bay coats gleamed as we slid the coffin on to the buggy.

I think Aunt Tilda would have smiled in gentle pleasure if she could have seen her funeral. Maybe she could. It was a fine one. We walked beside the buggy towards the grove of trees where my mother's grave lay regally in the shadows, and the mourners followed, two by two, behind us.

I heard their rich melodious voices break into a sweet hymn that swelled and ebbed in the way only coloured folks can make music and it filled my heart to bursting with the sad beauty of it. A grave had been dug, not far from my mother's, and the mourners clustered around it while we lowered the heavy casket into its depths. The rich red earth was piled high on each side and it gave off a smell of freshness and summer rain and new growth, in spite of the death it represented.

I began to feel bad again, while the minister intoned some prayers and read from his Bible. I never heard a word he said. From the corner of my eye I could see the pale gleam of the marble headstone on my mother's grave and once I looked up and caught Abe's gaze. His look was hard and malevolent. My brain was getting dizzy and, God help me, my throat was burning with the need. Somewhere, in the background, a woman was wailing high and hopeless and I think it was Salena, because I could hear Jed comforting her. While a new hymn was being sung, Jed and I and the other hands took up the spades that lay behind the grave and we began to fill in the dark hole at the bottom of which lay all that remained of Aunt Tilda.

Those first few spadefuls of earth were like a desecration, landing with irreverent scatchings on the polished lid of the casket, then the grave began to fill and pretty soon we had a neat, shaped mound, there in that grove of trees, and even that was hidden, soon, by the flowers, the women strewed on it. I went quickly, then, leaving the mourners still scattered around that place, because I sure as hell couldn't stand any more and I had to get away, whatever they thought of me. I fancied Ilse's eyes bored into my back as I went.

I knew where I was going and what I wanted, but I couldn't control it any longer. It was that or go crazy, I guessed, so I went back to the deserted Big House and in the coolness of Abe's living-room I crossed to the liquor cabinet and took up an opened bottle of whisky that stood there, slipped it under my coat and went outside again. I looked around me for a moment, making up my mind. There were a few folks wandering back from the grave, but I didn't much care if they saw me or not, they were still a ways off, and my need was chewing into me. One of the barns stood dark and empty and inviting, with its door open, so I made my way over to it and went inside. It was clean, smelling of hay and the lingering sweetness of horses, and a few chickens scratched about on the floor, chuckling to themselves. They fluttered agitatedly out of my way as I crossed to the wooden ladder that led to the loft and I took out the whisky bottle and held it in one hand as I climbed the rungs leading up to the privacy of that hay-filled landing.

So, that's where I spent the afternoon, quietly and alone, getting drunk stupid on that whisky of Abe's, toasting him and my misery and Aunt Tilda with every gulp I took, hating one and loving the other and filling myself with self-pity and loathing. Pretty soon, it paid off. The blackness came over me and I knew merciful nothing for a while.

I don't know for how long I was passed out, but it was growing dark with evening. Something began forcing me from sleep. I was half buried in the thick straw, my fingers still tight clenched around the neck of the bottle and there wasn't much left in it, maybe a pull or two. Someone had my shoulder and was shaking it vigorously, which set my head to pounding and my stomach to feeling sick.

I said, 'Go to hell,' thickly, and the smell of whisky was heavy around me. 'Let me sleep,' and I sank back in the hay, not knowing who shook me.

'Mister Saul, Mister Saul.' The grip on my shoulder was firmer, 'Are you all right?'

I snarled, 'For Chris'sakes, leave me alone!' Opened my eyes and sat up. The movement sent a fresh jolt of pain through my head and I groaned. Blinking, trying to focus my vision, I saw Salena's face swim into view. She was still clutching my shoulder and her face was anxious and concerned.

'It's you,' I said stupidly, the words slurring together.

'I saw you come in here, Mister Saul, after the buryin'. You been gone so long, I started in to worryin'.' Her dark innocent eyes held mine and I thought how pretty she was. And how young.

'I'm all right.' I spoke each syllable slowly, to get the words out right.

'You lookin' mighty sick. You want the doctor, Mister Saul?'

'Doctor?' I shook my head, gazing at her owlishly, 'Why?'

She indicated the bottle in my hand, 'You got the medicine with you. Same as you was lookin' for when you come to pa's place. You remember, that time when you had a bad stomach?'

She must have inherited her sweetness from Aunt Tilda. I laughed a little. 'This, sweet Salena, is the only doctor I need. I get enough of this, I'll never be sick again.'

She asked a little shyly, 'You want me to he'p you down?'

I shook my head, 'No, honey, I'm staying here till I've taken all my medicine.' The words sounded right in my head but they came out all wrong, halting and stumbling over each other, falling over my thick tongue and the bad taste in my mouth. I needed to wash it away, so I uncorked the bottle and took another pull at the liquid in it. It burned like fire and I doubled over, with my head bowed, so she couldn't see my ravaged face. I muttered, 'You'll never know, Salena, just how low-down rotten I am. Tilda dying there and me away, doin' those sinful things.'

'Oh, Mister Saul, don't take on so.' Salena came on to her knees beside me, her eyes liquid with unshed tears, 'I know how you feel about Gran'ma, but it weren't no doin' of yours. You didn't know she was dyin'.'

'I had no right to be away. No right.'

She said, like a woman crooning to a baby, 'There, there,' and suddenly she was older than I, warm and comforting and good to be near. Her soft brown arms stole out and cradled my head to her young, swelling breasts and I was content to let her hold me. I stayed there and in a moment my own arms reached out for her and drew her close and I murmured in her ear, 'You're a good girl, Salena.' And that was the way Jed found us, in each other's arms.

We didn't hear him come, because I was too drunk and Salena had started in to crying a little again, partly out of pity for me and partly through missing Tilda. I saw his head come over the edge of the landing and his eyes grew fierce and red as he saw us. The drink had dulled my reflexes, so I was slow in thrusting Salena from me. She gave a gasp at my roughness and I struggled to rise as Jed came on to the loft, his face twisted in the dim light from the cobwebbed window, his arms hanging long, held a little way from his sides, his fists bunched. He said, his voice a little cracked with burning emotion, 'Get up, Salena.' His eyes never left my face.

'You've got this wrong, Jed,' I was scrambling in the hay, trying to find my feet.

'Shut up, you bastard.' His eyes flickered to the empty bottle, lying with the last of its contents leaking into the hay. 'You drunken, randy, child-laying whoreson.'

Salena gave a little cry, his meaning at last coming to her. 'Pa!' She was standing up, now.

Jed didn't look at her, 'Get on home. I'll tend to you later.'

'But, Pa, he never—'

'Git!' The menace in his voice made her eyes larger than ever. Without another word, she turned and scurried down the ladder. We heard her bare feet cross the barn floor and then there was silence.

'Now, you,' Jed's hands clenched and unclenched at his sides and he spoke through his teeth. 'You're shit!'

I staggered to my feet, swaying and sick. 'Goddam, Jed. What do you think I am?'

'I know what you are. Or I thought I did. But you're worse than that. Worse than any of us thought—'

I started to speak but he broke in, stepping forwards a little, 'Over Ma's fresh grave, over her wasted, dead body, you'd try to take my girl?'

I said thickly, 'You're wrong, Jed. I told you. You're wrong.'

He snarled, 'You think Abe'd care if I killed you? He sets more store by me than he ever did on you. He'd be glad, you son of a bitch. And now, I'm going to take your head off.'

I saw him coming and tried to sidestep, but it was hopeless. I might as well have tried to stop an onrushing train. And it felt as though one had hit me. I went down with the first blow and he came down with me, throwing punch after punch while I raised my arms, trying to ward him off. Something wouldn't let me hit him back, and it wasn't the feebleness brought on by drink. I couldn't I guess, because I felt I deserved it. Not for his reasons, for my own.

I felt my lips split and a tooth go as his bunched fist hit my mouth, and I spat blood as he connected with my cheekbone. That opened, too, and I felt warmth running down my face to collect with the blood pouring from my broken mouth.

I didn't say anything, just grunted as the bull-force of his blows caught me in the stomach two or three times. I doubled for protection, winded, every muscle and bone in me screaming agony. He hit me in the face again and I tried to writhe away. At the same time I could hear a strange keening sound. There was only one eye I could open, the other was full of blood and as I rolled around, I saw him. He was drawing back his fist for a final blow and his mouth hung open and slack. The keening sound was coming from him and in the mist of pain and shock that surrounded me, I felt a numbing surprise to see the tears that coursed down his dark face.

That last blow never fell. He stood looking down at me, shaking his head and crying like a kid. Instead, he used the back of his hand, bruised and bloodied, to wipe his nose. I could only gasp for breath and peer at him out of my one good eye, lying there huddled at his feet. With a sudden savage movement he bent swiftly and I flinched openly, expecting the bone shattering impact, but instead he picked up that empty whisky bottle and hurled it viciously from him, away into the darkness, over the edge of the loft. Dimly, I heard it shatter on the floor beneath us.

Jed sniffed, wiping at his tears with stained fingers then looked down at me. 'You poor miserable bastard,' he said at last. 'You're no good to anyone and a damn sight less good to yourself. I guess there's no hope for you.'

He turned away then, the only brother I'd known and went down the ladder. I lay there listening to his shuffling, listless footsteps as he left the barn and I knew I'd lost him, too.

CHAPTER ELEVEN

I DIDN'T move until it was quite dark, and then, aching and stiff, I climbed down from the loft and went out. There was a trough of drinking water for the horses there and I stopped to clean myself some. I could just see out of my swollen eye and the water hurt like hell as its coldness touched me. I rinsed my mouth and spat out what remained of my tooth then made my way across the deserted yard to the corral where the gelding was waiting. My saddle and bridle hung over the rail, where I had left them that morning, so I called him over and put on his harness, mounted up and left the ranch.

There was no place else to go, I guess, except over to Abbie's. She wasn't there, so I unsaddled the gelding and let him go on her patch of ground. I couldn't call it a garden, it was so overgrown with grass and weeds. The gelding thought it was fine. He started in to grazing straight away, swishing his tail and making small sounds as he pulled at the grass. I climbed up on the porch and sat in the rickety old swing to wait for Abbie, letting the pain wash over me in tides, thinking about Tilda being gone and now Jed.

I slept a little and then Abbie came home. It was late and she had a man with her. He was kind of drunk, hanging on her arm for support, laughing as he stumbled beside her. I guessed she had been over to the saloon, looking for someone to give her some grubstakes. When they saw me sitting there, they both stopped. Abbie freed herself from the stranger's grip.

She said, 'You back so soon?'

I nodded, 'Uh-huh.'

'I'm sorry, feller. I'm already spoken for.' She pushed her companion. 'You come back another night. I'm going to be busy.'

He stared at her then at me, owlishly. 'But you said—'

'Never mind, honey. I got company.' Abbie's voice was impatient. 'You can see that, can't you? I got a visitor.'

'Well,' he hesitated, 'Well, sure.'

She turned her back on him and came up on the porch to me. I saw her bend to look at me. In the moonlight, I could see the frown on her face, so she must have seen the state my own was in. She shook her head. 'Trouble, that's all you find, Saul Bowen—' She held out her hand to me and I took it, coming to my feet. 'Come inside,' she said softly. Behind us, her would-be customer shuffled his feet, cleared his throat then went slowly away.

Inside, I sat limply on the bed while Abbie busied herself lighting the lamp. As its yellow glow filled the room she turned to look at me.

'Land's sakes! You're worse than I thought. Who'd you tangle with?'

I said, lopsidedly because of my torn mouth, 'It doesn't matter.'

'I know for sure it ain't Tolley. How many folks you goin' to rile so bad they want to kill you?' There was a sort of fond desperation in her voice. She had started fetching sponges and water in a bowl.

I said, 'I washed up.'

'Not near well enough. You're a mess, you.' She started to dab at my face and I winced and moved my head.

'Hold still,' she said sharply. After a while she seemed satisfied with her work. 'I guess you'll mend.' She started to clear away the bowl of pink-tinged water and the blood-stained sponges. 'You think you can be still a while and keep out of any new fights for a couple of days?'

'That's why I came,' I tried to grin. 'You're peaceful company.'

She was pleased, I could tell, and I knew, for a little while at least, I'd have somewhere to lay my head and rest up before the decisions that had to be faced came crowding at me and forced me on to God knew where.

I stayed with Abbie more than a couple of days. A week passed, peacefully and quietly and I almost enjoyed being alone with her. I had a little money with me, so I gave her that as I knew she would find it hard not being able to work while

I was around. She accepted it easily and naturally and I thought, wryly, she was used to taking her money from men. It wasn't much as I had left almost everything back at the ranch and it nagged at me that sometime, soon, I'd have to go back and pick up the rest of the money I had left. I pushed the notion away, putting it off, because I'd have to face Ilse's reproachful eyes. The thought of Ilse gave me an odd ache in the gut and a strange loneliness stole over me, so that I looked at Abbie in a new way and noticed her shabbiness, and the coarseness of her speech and the rough, gutter-level of her behaviour from time to time. But she was what she was and inside her there was a generous warmth that I had no right to ignore. All the same she began to bore me and I itched for action.

I couldn't stay here forever, trying to come to a decision. The move had to be made now, and then I could go on, triumphant or not, it made no never mind, so long as I tried. Abe had to be brought down. I was a man grown and sick of feeling his domination. I ached to win.

I watched Abbie moving around, one day, the seeds of impatience growing in me like a cancer. She was unaware of my study and the ideas running through my head, happily busy.

I said, 'You want to go someplace tonight?'

She paused, looking at me, smiling, 'Sure.'

'You want to meet my Pa?'

'What?' I saw the feelings chase across her face, surprise, hesitation then a certain eagerness. It occurred to me she might be considering that I was going to do the right thing; introduce her to my folks and then, God help us, make an honest woman of her! I almost choked, but held on to my control. Let her think what she wanted to. It was no fault of mine if she were fool enough to hope I'd ever settle down. No, Abbie, I thought, it's Abe I want to hurt. You'll be my tool.

'I guess it's time I went to see him. And step-ma. I guess we'll have dinner there. Ilse said I was to bring you.'

'Bring me?' her eyes held undisguised delight. 'Why, Saul, I didn't know you had spoken about me.'

'Sure I have, Abbie. I'm proud of you.' I put a false warmth in my voice and watched her eager reaction.

'My, won't that be wonderful?' She came to me and put her arms around me and tried to kiss my mouth, but I gave her my cheek. She was too excited to notice. 'Honey, there ain't one of the girls at the saloon ever been invited to a lady's house. Not a one! Won't they be just mad! They'll pretend they don't care, but I know they will.' She quietened, holding my hands in hers, her eyes searching mine, 'It's what we all dream about, but it never comes true, Saul. Bein' asked to meet a man's folks—I can't hardly believe it. I'm lucky, real lucky. You know that?'

I said, 'No, Abbie. You're a nice girl, that's all. I like being with you.' I didn't want things to get out of hand, but they were heading that way, where Abbie was concerned.

She started to flutter in the way women do about what she would wear, and how to fix her hair. She kept asking me fool questions and I was short with her at first, annoyed by her excitement, then began to consider. I'd help her pick her clothes with pleasure. I said, 'Wear your red dress.'

A small doubt showed. 'Ain't that too bright, honey?'

I put an arm around her waist. 'Can't be too bright on you. It makes you look beautiful. Wear it for me.'

She relaxed, 'If you like it, I sure will.'

I turned away, thinking bitterly that with any luck she'd wear feathers, too.

Abbie didn't wear feathers, but she wore too much cheap perfume, and the red dress looked just the way I wanted it to; too short, showing her ankles and too low, showing her pushed-up breasts so that they threatened to spill over the top. She looked like what she was and I was satisfied.

She grumbled a little because we didn't have a buggy and the gelding had to carry us both. I said, on the way, her perfume so heady it made me dizzy, 'Don't you fret, Abbie. Some day soon, we'll have us a buggy to ride in that will make the girls' eyes pop, you'll see. Over to the ranch, my Pa's got one drawn by Morgan bays that's the finest in the state.'

'I seen it,' she said breathlessly. 'Oh, Saul, you think one day we can ride in that?'

'Sure, honey.' I should have felt guilty, but I had more compelling urges that were nothing to do with her.

She leaned back in my arms, content, as the gelding made his way with us up the trail towards home.

Darkness had fallen by the time we reached the ranch, but it still showed up big and splendid as moonrise showed over the hills. The silvered pastures lay huge and spacious, dotted by the dark shapes of grazing mares and sleeping foals, and the workers' shacks and the low white shape of the Big House lost none of the impressiveness they held by moonlight. Abbie gave little squeals of delight as we passed each new sight, and she shivered a little as the Big House loomed in front of us. I was glad we were almost unnoticed, with few workers around and relieved there was no sign of Jed or Salena. I had guessed they would be in at their evening meal.

I pulled in, in front of the Big House, and hitched the gelding, then turned to help Abbie down. At the same time, the front door opened, throwing a square of yellow light across the porch and Ilse stood framed in the doorway. Her face was in shadow and I could not see her reaction, but after the first sudden stillness, her soft voice said, 'Saul. I'm glad you're home.'

I reached up for Abbie and helped her down, then held one of her hands as I turned to Ilse. 'This is Abbie. I told you about her.'

'Yes,' she came on to the porch towards us. If Abbie's crude dress taste and her strong perfume had thrown Ilse, she didn't show it. I had to hand it to her, she was a lady. 'I'm so glad to meet you, Miss Abbie.'

Abbie stepped away from me and went to Ilse, holding out her hand. 'I seen you so often, Miz Bowen,' Her voice was high and breathless, 'But I never thought I'd ever come visitin'. It was Saul, here, said you'd asked I should come to dinner and I can't tell you how proud I am. I just can't.' She ended with a nervous titter and Ilse looked past her at me.

'Why, you are both welcome.' Her eyes were masked with darkness. I went up the steps on to the porch to join them and Ilse reached and took my hand in greeting. 'I'm glad to see you,' her fingers were warm and gentle and I squeezed them, suddenly, and then let mine slide along hers because I was aching again, and wondering what the hell I was trying to do.

Ilse stilled at my touch, then took her hand away, but I saw the light catch her eyes for a moment, and they looked very big and wary. 'Abe is home,' she said.

'I hoped so,' I answered, 'I want him to meet my girl.' There was a barrier between us again.

Abbie fidgeted, bright as a butterfly and cheap as her perfume.

'I'm sure he will be glad,' Ilse's voice held the smallest tremor and I began to feel a surge of confidence. Now, Abe, I thought, let's shock you some more. How do you like it in your own home?

Ilse led the way in and I followed her, pulling Abbie's hand on to my arm. I could feel her fingers shaking. My boots were loud on the polished floorboards and I brought down my heels hard, standing tall.

Abe stood with his back to the fireplace, his hands clasped behind his back, his legs apart. The look on his face was harsh and unsmiling. Ilse said softly, 'Abe, Saul has brought his girl to meet us. Her name is Miss Abbie.' She turned and held out her hand to Abbie and drew her forward. 'This is Saul's father, Mister Bowen, Abbie.'

For a moment, I thought Abbie was going to curtsey, she was so awed and so impressed. Instead, she held out her hand for Abe to shake it. He hardly glanced at her, his eyes were full on me and they glittered.

'So, you came back,' he said harshly.

I smiled, pushing down the sudden stillness that had come over me. I was here to fight. 'Thought sure you'd like to meet my lady.'

Abbie had dropped her hand and was using it to smooth down the flounces on her skirt, a little unsure now. Abe ignored her. 'Yes,' he said, but there was nothing in his voice but belligerence.

Ilse spoke, nerves tingeing her words, 'Saul would like to stay and eat with us.'

Abe did not move. 'You owe us a week's work and more. There are no wages coming to you.' His eyes held mine, cold and hostile.

'I still got money,' I smiled again.

'Then buy your meal elsewhere.'

'Abe!' Ilse looked unhappily from one to the other of us. 'There is more than enough for all of us.'

For a while longer, Abe glared at me, then his eyes turned to Abbie. At last, he bowed his head slightly in her direction, 'As you wish.'

That was one small round I had won. I relaxed a little, still eager to push my advantage.

Ilse went away, to fix more vittles and prepare more places at the table, I guess, and Abe stayed where he was, looking at us coolly. It was up to me. I took Abbie's arm and led her to a chair. 'You sit there honey, and I'll fix you a drink.' Not looking at Abe, I went to his store of liquor and picked a bottle of good French brandy. I could feel his eyes boring into my back. I poured drinks and heard Abbie begin to chatter, suddenly, her words fast and tumbling. 'My, Mister Bowen, I never seen any place so splendid. Saul sure is lucky to live here. And I'm sure lucky to visit with you and your wife. I really do appreciate it.'

I turned and handed her a glass almost full of neat brandy and took one myself. I said to Abe, 'You?' and he shook his head.

Abbie, unknowing, tossed back the brandy as though it were the cheap redeye she was used to and started in to gasping and choking so that I stepped over to her and hit her on the back. She spluttered a little. I laughed, 'Take it easy honey, that's good stuff.'

'Sure is. My, I never tasted so fine.'

'Have another.' I refilled her glass and she drank that too, too quickly. With the strength of the drink flooding through her, she became flushed and excited and started to prattle. She repeated over and over how proud she was to be here, 'You must be real rich, Mister Bowen, real rich,' and couldn't seem to recover from the excitement of the size of the spread and how well it was doing, 'We all admire you in town, you're a big man to us. Wish we saw more of you.'

I refilled her glass two or three times, then saw she was becoming drunk, rapidly. Hell, she wasn't going to get there before me. I drained some more brandy, then turned to another bottle of Abe's good Scotch. We began to drink that, together. Abe said nothing, watching us silently, his face taut and hard and a small muscle twitching high in his cheek. I was enjoying myself. Because I wanted to be, I was already half drunk, and Abbie's voice, slurring a little, showed her own state. She was saying, 'It's so good to have Saul around, you don't know! He's a real man, Mister Bowen. There's not many girls in the saloon can say they've been fought over, but he fought for me. Did you hear about it?' Abe's eyes never left my face. 'Why, he almost killed a man because of me. I was so proud! He sure don't back down, Saul. Why, that Tolley fell almost dead when Saul shot him, so much blood and all, I felt sure he'd die. But, no sir, he knows when he's beat. Why,' she hicupped and I gave her another drink, 'why, when that sheriff come lookin' for Saul, ol' Tolley said he'd got no complaints. Ain't that wonderful?'

I gazed into Abe's expressionless eyes and felt my mouth quirk at the corner. Pouring some more liquor into my glass, I held it up and silently toasted Abe, over Abbie's head. His look became stony and I gave a small laugh, then clutched at the back of Abbie's chair as the room suddenly dipped and swayed.

'Whooh,' I said, 'Hold hard, Abbie, Abe can't take so much in, he's so proud of me.'

'Well, I don't blame you, Mister Bowen, I surely don't. I'm so proud of Saul, too.' Abbie turned to me, holding out her glass, 'Pour me some more of that there drink, honey. It's a whole lot better than what we have over to my place.'

I don't know when Ilse had joined us. I hadn't seen her enter, but she stood watching us, trying to hide her dismay. 'The meal is ready,' she said quietly.

I moved to Abbie and tripped, lurching over her, the whisky bottle still in my hand. I gave her my arm to lead her in to dinner and that excited her, too. We went in where Ilse had prepared places for us and Abbie made excited noises about the food. I guess she was hungry, we didn't eat much at her place, preferring to drink. As we sat down, I filled more glasses with whisky, and she was already drinking when Ilse started to say grace. I felt a small twinge of guilt as Ilse's voice trailed away in discomfort noting Abbie's oblivion to anything but the food in front of her.

She talked a stream of inanities through the meal, dropping her knife and spilling a little of the drink down her dress, leaving a dark stain on the bright red satin. Abe ate hardly anything, picking at his food, saying nothing. Ilse tried to smile a couple of times but failed. Me, I matched Abbie drink for drink, not eating much, getting high and feeling strangely down. I guess I had had enough too, when Abe put a stop to it. He rose and came around the table to us, standing tall and stern and hostile.

'I've been glad to meet you, Miss Abbie,' he said, 'and to know a little more about Saul.' His face turned to me. 'Sometimes, I wonder how he has survived for so long.' He paused, then returned to Abbie, 'I think you are not too well, perhaps he should take you home.'

Abbie nodded happily, clinging to me, 'I'm real proud,' she said again.

To me, Abe said, 'Your things are still upstairs. I suggest you fetch them soon.' Then he went away, out of the room.

I guess I had succeeded. I had shocked and humiliated him, and that was what I wanted to do, but I wondered why I didn't feel better about it. There was no elation in me, just a flat, dull feeling of anticlimax. Ilse said nothing and I didn't look at her as I helped Abbie, grinning and not really knowing much, away from there.

CHAPTER TWELVE

I WASN'T too happy about things on the way back. My small triumph had turned out to be my biggest loss. Maybe I shouldn't have expected it to be any other way. I swayed in the saddle, trying to hold on to Abbie and keep her in place at the same time. She was worse than I was, but I was pretty bad too. Once we both fell off and the gelding, his patience tried sorely, tried to move on, but I had one arm caught in the rein so he didn't get far. It took some time getting back in the saddle, and Abbie thought it was funny. She giggled a lot and I was tired of her. The drink hadn't dulled the ache in me at the thought of my failure and couldn't stop me from knowing what I had to do.

I could hardly wait to tumble Abbie into the bed in her shack. She lay fully dressed across it, at an angle and fell asleep at once, smiling to herself. I didn't bother to make her comfortable, but stepped outside once more, staggering a little, and rolled a smoke, leaning against a doorjamb, coming to a decision.

I'd be sorry to leave Abbie, but not too sorry. I was finished here, that was sure, and there were no more strings to draw me back; no Tilda, no Jed, not even Abe. It seemed strange to admit that he had been the strongest magnet for me, but he had been. I could face that now, and it was a kind of relief to do it, but even then I couldn't understand why, or which was the most powerful reason, my hate for him and desire to win at all costs, or, God help me, my love and need for my father. I shrugged and felt a lump in my throat which I didn't understand either. I guess it was the drink.

I wondered if Abbie would know why I hadn't said goodbye to her. That was as difficult for me as any hello. I had never said either word to anyone, except for Tilda.

Without looking back, I heaved myself into the saddle again and took the trail, still a little drunk, heavy-spirited.

The Big House was in darkness, silent and forbidding. My heart began to pound, now that I was here again. I was impatient to get it over with, to climb those stairs, collect my things and get the hell out. For good.

The door creaked a little as I opened it, the sound loud in the darkness, and I felt like a thief, sneaking in the silence. The stairs creaked too, as I put my weight on them, and I clung to the banister feeling my way up. On the landing, a shaft of moonlight showed me the way, and in my room the silvery beams through the window were as good as lamplight.

I bundled all I felt I would need into my saddle-bags, checking the rest of my money and my gun were still there, in one of them, then hung them over my arm and went out. The stairs creaked again as I descended them, and I cursed silently to myself at the unnecessary noise. I was almost down when I heard a sound and the landing above me became awash with pale light. I turned, cold with unreasoning panic and looked up. Ilse stood there, carrying a lamp, dressed in a full white robe that made her look like a Grecian priestess. Her face was pale, her eyes dark in the light from the lamp.

She whispered, 'Saul, where are you going?'

I turned and descended the last stairs, and she came after me, her robe's hem whispering on the steps as she moved.

'Saul,' she said again.

I turned as she caught up with me. 'Away,' I said harshly. 'I'm finished here. It was a waste of time.'

'No!'

Suddenly I was angry. How much convincing did she need? I dropped my saddle-bags, took the lamp from her and set it on a table, then took her gently by the shoulders. 'Ilse, it wasted your time, and mine and Abe's. You wanted us to be the kind of people we can't be. Accept it now. You tried and we all failed.'

She said nothing, pale and sad, and I was sad too, for her, for me. Her shoulders under my hands were small and warm and suddenly that feeling came over me again, stronger than ever, crazy. My fingers tightened on her and there was a quick awareness in her eyes, a sort of fear. I pulled her towards me and I heard her gasp and I tilted my head and kissed her roughly and deeply on the mouth.

She was as tight as a drawn bowstring, tense and trembling a little. I could feel her trying to pull away, but that devil in me held her back, closer in my arms, against my body and then she stilled, perhaps admitting to herself, at last, that there was more in this than just Abe and me and our enmity.

When I let her go, she stepped back, no longer frightened, her eyes calculating. 'Was that for goodbye?' she asked a little tremulously, 'Or is it still the drink?'

Fury exploded in my head. 'Maybe I'm drunker than I thought,' I snapped at her, and reached, dragging her close. She made no sound and did not fight as I took her mouth again, pushing her against the banister forcing her lips apart.

God knows how long he had been standing there, at the top of the stairs, watching us, but Abe gave a kind of broken roar, then, and began to come down towards us. We parted and stared at him in a kind of dazed horror as he roared again, and I recognised the distorted sound as my name. I wish he could have looked ridiculous in those long white underpants and the undershirt buttoned up to his throat. His hair was awry and his eyes flamed, dark holes with hell in them and all he had was a kind of awful dignity.

He reached the bottom of the stairs and kept coming towards us and beside me Ilse stirred and moved away, her face white with guilt and fright. She tried to speak but no sound came from her while he advanced on me. I couldn't move.

He stopped at last, as tall as I, wide and dark and menacing. His mouth worked. 'You took one wife from me, you devil's spawn, and now you're trying to take the other. I'll see you dead first.'

My stomach turned and the years fell away and suddenly he was bigger than I was and my life rose up in my throat, thick as a bile, to choke me and I heard my own voice, weak, cry out, 'Pa!' The first time in twenty years I had used that word.

'Don't call me that. Don't ever call me that,' the hatred

hissed between his lips. 'You belong to no one and never will.'

But I was grown now, and had to make a stand. So out of the fear that was still in me, and the hopelessness and the hurt of it all I shouted something I don't remember and pushed him in the chest, with both hands, mostly to get him away from me, to move out of his shadow. He stumbled back towards the fireplace and caught his heel in the rug, fetching up against the wall with a solid blow that drove the breath from him. I heard it escape between his lips, and his face turned white with murder blazing from his eyes.

Behind me, Ilse gave a little cry, and then Abe turned, quick and light, and in one swift, easy movement he had one of those rifles off the wall and was pointing it right at me. He snarled, then, like an animal, and said, 'From the day you killed your mother these hung here to remind me what you are. I never forgot. It's a fitting end for you and there's none will blame me!' His voice had risen as control left him and I saw his finger begin to tighten on the trigger.

I don't know why I wanted to save myself. There wasn't much reason, but it was instinct, I guess. I moved at the same time as that gun muzzle came up and jerked with the concussion and I heard the bullet tear past as I threw myself at Abe. There was a dull, heavy sound as the bullet embedded itself in the wall and then I caught Abe around the knees and he crashed to the floor on his back. His face was twisted and almost inhuman as his head rested against the fender of the fireplace and, if anything, his hate was even deeper. My heart raced against my ribs and my breathing was short and gasping, my head swimming. I knew for sure, now, he'd kill me. He wanted me dead, my father Abe.

I didn't see his hand reaching for the poker, but he must have grasped it while I crouched over him, mesmerised by the hypnotic evil in his eyes, sick to my stomach at this final showdown. When he hit me, I thought he had succeeded at last. The poker came slashing across my ear and the side of my head with a skull-shattering impact that threw me sideways and stunned me motionless for a moment. I heard my own groan coming from somewhere far away and, mercifully, there was no feeling from that side of my head, though I could feel the warmth of blood trickling. I guessed the pain would come later, if I lived, but for now I saw Abe reach down deliberately for the rifle that had fallen from his hands. Slowly and certainly he broke it open and reached for the box of shells he kept on the shelf. From my position on the floor, I watched in disbelief as he slipped another cartridge into the breech then snapped the gun shut.

Abe sure as hell meant it. There was only one way out for me and I took it. He must have thought I was more stunned than I was, because he was taken by surprise. I rolled and came to my knees with a speed that amazed even me, but I was fighting for my life now. As he levelled the gun at me again, I was on it, twisting the barrel up and away from me, wrenching that godawful weapon from his grasp. I fell back with it and reversed it, as he howled and came towards me and Ilse shrieked somewhere in the gathering darkness around us. The butt of the rifle was in my hip, my finger was on the trigger, the barrel wavered somewhere between Abe's chest and his stomach and then the gun exploded, horrifyingly, the kick of it sending me thrashing backwards, caught off balance and in a panic while Abe flew once more against the wall, but this time propelled by greater force than I could control.

I heard Ilse shriek again and there was a dull pounding in my head and a dizzy, wild singing in my ears. At that range the bullet had done terrible damage to Abe's chest. He had slid down the wall leaving red, glistening streaks along it and the once white front of his undershirt was black with powder burns and splattered with blood and torn flesh. Oh my God, my own father! And in my hands was the gun that had killed my mother. I couldn't move or think or even feel for a while, just sat there where I had fallen and looked at Abe's already glazing eyes, still filled with murder and hate. It flashed through me that when they closed his eyes, they would shut the lids over that terrible emotion, and it would stay there forever, hidden.

Slowly, I became aware of Ilse's sobbing. She was on her hands and knees, her face twisted with an agony of horror and shock. She was saying, 'Abe, Abe,' staring at him, willing him to be alive and knowing it was hopeless. Then she rose and went across the room to him and went down on her knees again, reaching for that poor bloodied body, pulling his head to her chest and rocking him back and forth like a mother with a child.

I got to my feet and stood there, drained and exhausted, looking at her with that gun still in my hands. She seemed to come to her senses for a moment. Her eyes focused on me, hard with dread as she hissed, 'Go, Saul. Go now. I can do no more for you.'

Like a sleepwalker, I moved forward to the mantelshelf, picked up the box of shells, and carrying that and the gun walked out of there without looking back. I didn't have to. That scene was emblazoned on my brain and only death will erase it.

As I came down off the porch, I saw shadowy figures coming from the workers' shacks so I unhitched the gelding quickly, climbed up on him and headed out, away from them, across Abe's pastures towards open country that I had never crossed before. I didn't know where in hell I was heading.

The moon was still out, silvering the quiet land. Bushes, dark and crouching, reached out at us as we fled past. The gelding was enjoying his run and stretched out low, hugging the ground. I was glad I had picked him for his speed. After a little while I began to feel light-headed and stupid, so I pulled him in, listening for sounds of pursuit, but there were none yet. Things began to get darker suddenly and I swayed in the saddle, so I dismounted quickly and, hanging on to the bridle, threw up in the bushes. It was a little easier after that, so I remounted and carried on.

I guess I hadn't really expected to hear the sounds of a chase. There was no trail to follow by night, but I knew first light would have them hot on my tail. I could picture it now. There would be someone sent to town to fetch Sheriff Byrnes, and a more than eager posse would soon be gathering at the ranch scanning the sky for the first signs of dawn so they could pick up my tracks. At daybreak, too, I'd have to think about covering the evidence of my flight. Right now, I could do nothing about it, being unfamiliar with this part of the country. I knew somewhere there should be rocky ground, or maybe even a river that would slow them up some and give me a chance.

The gelding was blowing, and I slowed to a walk, knowing now my life depended on him. In this darkness, too, a chance prairie dog hole could mean the end for both of us. He was grateful for the respite and it gave me a little time to think. I had just lit out, dazed with shock, with no supplies, no clothes, no plans and no idea where I was heading; nothing but the gun, a box of shells and a horse. It looked like this time I had outrun my luck, what little I had.

CHAPTER THIRTEEN

By the time the sky began to pearl in the East, we had gone a comfortable distance from the ranch, to my way of thinking. I knew any posse would cover the ground quicker than I had, helped by daylight. I guessed they were just starting out now, but it would still take time to find my tracks.

I thought about the Colt that I had left in my bags and wondered on the irony of my actions in putting it away never to be brought out while I stayed at the ranch. It would seem fate would see Abe dead by the gun whether I had hidden my own or not. There was no sense in regretting leaving the handgun and my saddle-bags behind—I hadn't given them a thought. The rifle was more than adequate with its greater range and accuracy, and I felt a kind of comfort in having it along even though I hated it and what it stood for—my mother's death and my father's, both at my own hands. Looking down at the damn thing as it lay across my arm it seemed to have a baneful life and purpose of its own. It gleamed dully in the early light, and seemed to pulsate, possessed by a spirit of evil.

Details of the countryside came into sharper focus with the gathering dawn. If I was on range land, it was disused and wild. Ungrazed, it stretched for miles around me and I guessed it belonged to no one. There were no trails, no signs of fencing. Far on the horizon was a dark uneven line of trees and beyond them a purpling range of hills. I headed towards them, wanting water and hoping there would be some near the trees. The gelding couldn't last long without it and his need was urgent.

The sun was well up and hawks were circling lazily by the time we were almost at the trees. They stretched in a shivering line of aspens, their leaves trembling in an unfelt breeze. The gelding became excited. He stretched his neck, grunted and broke into an unbidden trot. I felt my heart leap with the hope that he had smelled water and I wasn't disappointed. We burst through the undergrowth and lower branches and a stream lay there, sparkling and fresh and lonely, tumbling over pebbles, rushing away into the distance. The gelding headed, sliding, down the bank and into the water and pulled at the reins for me to release him to let him drink.

I slid from the saddle and stood beside him with the cool clear water running over my boots. While he drank slowly, I crouched and cupped my hands and took up the water and filled my mouth. It was so cold, it made my teeth ache. Standing, I looked upstream, trying to discern where it came from. It disappeared in winding banks, overhung with thick willows, sometimes narrow, sometimes wider, but coming from the direction of the now nearby hills. I could see the nearest one, crowned by naked grey rocks and the darkness of a chasm that ran crookedly up it. I guessed the stream came through it.

Finished drinking, the gelding raised his head and stood, head up, ears pricked, looking back the way we had come. I could hear nothing but my senses were no match for his. If he couldn't hear, he could certainly smell, or sense, something coming. I swore, not really believing that we were in any danger yet, but anxious, just the same, to be moving on. Looking back along the bank and the wilderness we had just passed through, I could see no sign of our trail, but there were hoofprints on the soft mud by the stream where the gelding had entered the water. Dragging him behind me, I went back to the spot and stood there a moment staring at the marks of his shoes.

The water chuckled around our legs and I could feel the coldness of it seeping into my boots through the cracking leather. Under our feet, the pebbles stirred and shifted, sending little clouds of disturbed sand in swirls to the surface. When I moved away, the pebbles fell back into place, forced home by the movement of the water, and it took only a few seconds for the stream bed to clear again. There'd be no trace left for long if we moved, in the water, upstream. With my mind made up, I reached forward and broke a branch from a low hanging bush and swept futilely at the hoof prints on the bank. They were deep and filling with water and the marks I made with the branch looked like what they were; an attempt to cover my tracks. Cursing, I looked around but there was nothing much I could do. The break in the branch was clean and new, showing fresh white wood where it had joined the parent bush. From where I was, the scar on the bush, too, showed all too plainly. At last, desperately, because time was wasting and I had to make the best of it, I stuck the splintered end of the branch in the bank, half burying it and lay the leaves across the tell-tale hoof prints. I hoped anyone passing above would see no more than a broken branch lying on the stream bank and make no more of it.

It couldn't be helped, so I turned, and dragging the gelding after me, began to make my way, on foot, upstream, wading through the fast running water. The willows were dense, and from time to time I had to force my way through them. Sometimes the gelding baulked, his eyes wide and white-edged, at a particularly wild spot, but tugging and cursing brought him on. I guess his feet were cold, but so were mine. My boots were less than useless. After a little time, the stream began to widen and deepen, the bottom shifting and treacherous so that I sank almost to my knees a couple of times. The edges were still tangled in undergrowth and I began to look for a place to leave the water for a little while. We were climbing steadily all the while, and I guessed we'd reached the lowest slopes of the hills.

Around noon, I found a tunnel of low-arched trees leading away from the stream around a barely discernible track. I guessed it was a game trail where deer came down to drink, and it suited my purpose. I pulled the gelding after me on to solid ground and we followed the track for maybe half a mile before it petered out altogether in thick undergrowth and trees. Sunlight filtered through the high green ceiling and began to dry my wet pants, but I could hear the water in my boots and my feet were sore and rubbing against the soaked leather. It wasn't long before I was limping. If I could have ridden in that crazy wilderness, I would have, but it was all I could do to find my way between the bushes and trees. As it was, I caused too much damage, brushing through broken branches and crushing fallen twigs underfoot. I didn't like to look back and see what kind of a trail I had blazed.

The gurgle of the stream sounded once more and I guessed I had moved in a wide semicircle. After the difficult passage I had just had, the thought of making my way through the water once more was almost pleasant. The gelding had rested enough from carrying me, so I planned to ride him this time. At least, he wasn't wearing boots, I thought grimly. We broke into bright sunshine then, and the stream, wide and shallow, was still running freely before us. The far banks, though, were open and flat stretching away and up towards the top of the rock-capped hills higher than they had looked.

Aching with the walking I had done, I turned to the gelding and mounted him and tried to push him back into the water, but he refused, shaking his head and switching his tail with irritation, tugging at the reins and putting his muzzle down towards the sweet, lush grass on the banks. I hadn't thought of his hunger, and now, with the idea in me, my stomach spoke loudly, so I dismounted again and let him graze for a while. I sat on a decaying stump and rolled a smoke from the makings in my coat pocket and watched him eat, wishing I ate grass, too.

Idly, I cast about for a berry bush thinking early summer was a bad time for berries then saw the small white flowers in the shorter grass high up the stream bank. Hopefully, they were wild strawberries, so I moved on over and found that they were. There were too many unripe ones, but there were enough to fill two fists and some to put in my pockets, for later. They would have to do till I could find some lonely habitation I could raid for food. If I had to hold someone at gunpoint, I guessed I'd do it.

While I was wandering around looking for more strawberries, I came across the lower slopes of a green lichen-covered rock that jutted out high, its top golden with sunlight. The gelding was happy to graze and fill his belly while he had the opportunity, so I laid the rifle at the foot of the rock and scaled it slowly, enjoying the warmth of its surface against my body. I sprawled my length against it, looking for hand and toe holds. It rose high as the trees, higher in some places, and I made for one of its peaks with some notion that I could make better plans if I saw how the country lay from its height.

It was a tougher climb than I had anticipated, and I was soon panting with heat and thirst, weakened as I was by hunger and the speed of my flight and no sleep at all. My eyes already felt gritty and bloodshot and I hoped I'd get some rest tonight, if only a few hours. It was then I stopped, my heart seemed to leap into my throat and a cold chill ran down my back. Far downstream, where the water was lost to view in the green wilderness, and the tops of the trees made a solid roof that looked like a curly carpet from my vantage point, a wisp of pale grey, almost colourless smoke rose in the still afternoon air.

Whoever it was, he or they were nearly in the same place I had entered the stream that morning. Someone had made a fire and had stopped for something to eat and coffee, I guess, before moving on. I wasn't fool enough to dismiss that as coincidence. Who the hell else would be in this lonely, godforsaken country if it wasn't the posse or part of it?

I felt sick and almost in despair while I sprawled out on that rocky height and gazed down and away at the steady plume of smoke.

Maybe, I thought, clambering down the rock, they hadn't found my tracks. Maybe I had lost them at the stream. If it was the posse, they had a damn good tracker with them to have caught up so easily, and it churned my stomach to think of my careless passage through the bushes after I had left the stream. There was only one thing and that was to take to the water again, make it fast, and head for the rocky hilltop, hoping I could lose them up there. My descent of the rock was easier and faster than my climb. I was careless and skinned my hands when I lost my footing, twisted my ankle painfully and ripped my pants' knees and the front of my coat. Crazy, I thought hopelessly, when they don't find my tracks on the far bank they'll know I took to the water. It's only a matter of time if they come upstream. If they go downstream, it's only a delay. I guessed they'd split up anyway. Maybe they were deciding that right now while they sat around and drank their coffee and discussed what a hunted man would do and put themselves in my shoes. Goddam their eyes!

My boots touched grass and my twisted ankle sent a bolt of pain up my shin to my knee. I picked up the rifle and limped over to the gelding. He had eaten his fill, and this time he was willing to carry me some more. We took to the water and he splashed his way upstream towards the hill crest quite happily. I urged him on to a faster walk and rode listening to the sounds of his hooves moving through the water and straining at the same time for other tell-tale noises, though I knew they were too far away for me to hear anything. I was almost dropping with fatigue and still as hungry as ever. The strawberries rammed into my pockets showed a red bloody stain on my coat and I put in my hand and crammed a fistful of the crushed fruit into my mouth. They made my juices run and I felt hungrier, my belly drawing in at the taste of them.

We moved on, into the later afternoon, and shadows began to grow long, dimming the stream and turning the silver of its sparkles golden. I could see those blessed tumbled rocks on the hilltop take shape and shadow, becoming individual boulders as we neared them. Some were as big as the rock I had climbed that afternoon, some no bigger than knee-high, but they lay scattered around and over each other, making crevices and caves and my impatience grew as I neared them.

Far behind me, dimmed by distance, but echoing from the valley below, I heard the sharp report of a gun. I wanted to fool myself into believing it wasn't a shot, but I knew what it was. It was probably a signal and someone, somewhere, had found something: a hoof-print, a broken branch. They were still coming and I hadn't shaken them off yet. I stopped then, pulling in the gelding and staring ahead at the hilltop. It would be faster to leave the water now and make a run for the rocks. I hoped I was far enough away and that the fading light was deceptive enough not to show my fleeting figure as I lit out.

With a sharp slap, I put the gelding at the bank and up, across the meadow, racing for the cover of the rocks. There was no sound of distant gunfire, so I guessed I was unobserved, and I reached them in a flurry of scattering small stones and a rise of dust from the gelding's hooves. Dismounting again, and wincing at the pain from my ankle, which was swollen, hot and throbbing inside my boot, I took the reins and pulled him in among the rocks. We wound our way, twisting, among them, and I knew for sure I'd left no trace. The ground was hard and stony. We climbed upwards as the world darkened and twilight came, grey and watchful. Sometimes the gelding held me back, refusing some difficult passage and I had to figure another way to get him along.

I was filled with a foreboding that he would slip and break a leg as the light worsened, and at last I had to stop. Though he slowed me down, I couldn't afford to be without him. Looking around, I found a kind of alcove that was set into the craggy hillside and guessed it would have to do. I forced him into it and followed him in, settled down against the hard wall of dry, weathered earth and rested at last.

CHAPTER FOURTEEN

THOUGH I was so played out, sleep was almost impossible. My brain whirled with fear, and the past came back to haunt me worse than ever, made more sickening by the memory of what I had done to Abe and how he had looked, lying bloody on the floor with Ilse crooning over him. It was the first time I had been able to think, and I wished I didn't have to. It was cold as night fell and the wind began to whistle among the rocks, making a moaning sigh that chilled my very being. My swollen foot was so agonising now, I felt an overwhelming need to take off my boot, but I knew that would be foolish. I was sure that I would never be able to put it on again in the morning and the thought of travelling on over that rough terrain shoeless was enough to make me settle back and cope with the pain as best I could.

I must have slept, though I don't remember drifting off, but suddenly I came to full awareness. The stars were out in the high, black velvet vault and the rocks around me were no more than deeper shades of darkness. The gelding stood where I had left him, but I could see his head high and his ears pricked in silhouette against the starlight and again I heard him make the noise that had awakened me. It was a gentle whicker and I came painfully to my feet, hobbled over to him and put a hand on his soft nose to quieten him. I strained my ears, trying to hear what had alerted him, and then it came to me; no sound, but the smell of smoke, wood smoke mixed with tobacco. My heart leaped again. Whoever it was, was near.

Quietly, I hitched the gelding's hanging reins under a rock, securing him, then I moved out into the darkness, taking one slow careful step at a time. I couldn't afford to slip, nor make a noise, but I had to find out for sure just who was smoking by a camp-fire. The rifle was a long, black shape, an extension of my hand, and I stopped for a moment to load it before I moved on.

There was a low glow away to my right, at the edge of the grasslands, where the rocky outcrop began. It would take me too far from my hiding place and the horse, but some compulsion moved me onward, noiselessly and sly as a coyote, every nerve and muscle tensed.

I moved around until the glow was hidden, knowing I would approach it from behind and, giving a small grunt of pain, I climbed up on to the first of the rocks and went down on my stomach. I wormed over them, drawing myself painfully over the granite, avoiding dips and hollows, hearing, sometimes, the tiny scrape of my boots on the hard surface. The sounds were so small they were lost in the sough of the night wind and I reached the place undetected. As I approached, I could see the glow of the fire again, lighting the surrounding rock face and I smelled the tang of coffee. It made my skin crawl with need. If it was one man, whoever he was, I'd take him for his coffee.

But it was more than one man. There were three of them, and I knew who they were. One of them was Sheriff Byrnes' deputy, the second was Tolley's friend from the saloon, and the third, blast him, was Tolley himself. It amazed me to see him so cocky and confident, sitting by the fire facing the rock I peered over. The other two were sitting in profile, occasionally leaning forward to poke at the fire and send its flames leaping upwards into the night. But it was Tolley who held my attention. His shirt was open, showing the white bandages at his waist, wads of them, layer upon layer, and his hands were cupped around a tin mug from which he sipped, but he was talking fast and low and the other two listened, nodding their heads from time to time, saying 'Yeah, Tolley', and 'Sure'. He always was a big mouth.

'I tol' you,' he said, 'he had to come up here. Byrnes says no, but I *feel* him. I can almost smell him. Smell his fear. I hunted enough animals, and men, too, to know what they smell like. He's around. Come morning, we'll know for sure.'

I ducked down and laid my head on my arms, cursing him and feeling sick again. I should have killed him that time. I should have. Maybe, now— I raised my head, bringing up the gun, but his friend spoke.

'Build up the fire some more, Byrnes won't see it from down there. I guess he didn't find any tracks the way he went or we'd have heard the signal.' Good naturedly, Tolley threw another branch on to the fire.

'See?' he murmured so I had to strain to hear him, 'we was the only ones found any tracks. If it wasn't for me, you'd be way back on the plains, still nosin' around.'

So it was Tolley. A hunting man, he would be a good tracker, too. He had been the one to put them on my trail. I guessed they had split up, only partly believing him, but he'd been right, and now he was here. I wondered how far away were the others and how much time I had. In the dark, they couldn't catch up with me, and in daylight, if Tolley wasn't there, it was likely they'd never find a trace. I had to move now. Say goodbye, Tolley, I got to finish what I started!

I lay the rifle across the rock to steady it, took a bead on Tolley's big, firelit face and pulled the trigger. The explosion rocked the night and echoed backwards and forwards on the rock strewn hillside. Tolley was down and messy, with no head left. Now, the deputy. He had risen, mouth open, handgun out, peering into the darkness towards my rock. Even in the glowing firelight I could see his face had a greenish pallor. I reloaded, he heard it and turned to run and I caught him full in the back. His body landed with a thud in the dust, way the other side of the flames. Tolley's friend was already up and running. He had burst into the shadows and was racing down the hill, but he had reckoned without the range of the rifle or how fast I could reload. I rammed home another bullet from my bulging pockets and hit him with ease. He disappeared without a sound, rolling over and over somewhere in the wild blackness. As the crashing echoes died down, I heard the fading sounds of birds, disturbed from their roosting places, calling in bewilderment as they flapped distractedly in the alien night sky.

I slid down from my rock, clutching the rifle, and limped over to the fire. There I kicked dirt over it until there was no flicker of life left, not even a smouldering ember. By starlight, I could see the coffee had been turned over and spilled, and I cursed about that, I could have done with some. Then I looked up and saw the distant wilderness dotted with firefly lights. The posse had lit torches and were headed this way. I grinned a little. They were probably falling over each other and panicking, trying to find each group down there among the trees. They had sure spread out, I could see them coming from all directions, and their yells were borne to me faintly, up here among the wind-singing rocks. Catch me, Byrnes, if you can. Come morning, I'll be long gone.

But it wasn't so easy. In the darkness, the horse posed more of a problem than he had when I could see which way to go. The posse didn't worry me too much for the moment, they were still falling over each other in the darkness down there in the trees and with no campfire to guide them, Tolley and his companions could have been anywhere. I decided, at last, I'd have to leave the horse. It wouldn't be any slower on foot among these rocks, and it would be easier to find someplace to hole up. Maybe, later, I'd catch up with him again. I unsaddled him, up there in the darkness, and took off his bridle and pushed the harness down under the cover of a rocky overhang. He stared at me in bewilderment, a shadow in the shadows, as I left him, climbing higher and away from him. I never saw him again.

The hills became silent once more, except for the keen of the night wind which blew stronger, whistling around my ears as I moved steadily away, trying not to heed the crashing yell of my ankle. My passage was clumsy and slow, but not as difficult as that of the pursuers behind me. They had something to look for and find, but I had only one purpose and that was to put as much distance between them and myself as possible.

I kept going, pausing now and again to listen but heard nothing that alarmed me too much. The starlit rocks loomed around me, waiting and watching as I moved among them. An occasional pebble slid back from my straining boots and rattled, echoing, down the hillside, but only for a little way.

The weight of the ammunition in my pockets was comforting, the means of my salvation.

Now I reached the hilltop. In the dim starlight I saw a wide pasture run down into a shadowed valley and start up again the other side to a new, higher hill. This one was dressed in trees and gullies and more rocks. If I could reach it, there would be some place to go to earth among its safe-seeming recesses. Looking behind me once more and seeing and hearing no sounds of pursuit, I broke into a hurried, awkward run, praying I wouldn't do any more damage to my injured foot. I should have known better, I guess. Some snag, down in the tall, whispering grass, caught at my boot heel and I lost my footing, feeling my legs go out from under me. There was the dew-wet, spiky prickle of grass under my cheek and the dampness of it soaking my clothes as I rolled down the hillside, desperately keeping a tight hold on the rifle as I careered down into the blackness of the valley, fetching up, at last, against a fallen tree bole. For a moment I lay there, winded, my breathing short and fast, and that ankle of mine throbbing with renewed agony.

It must have sounded like the passage of a wounded buffalo, and it seemed to me that the dying echoes of my fall were laced with new, far away but progressively louder sounds. I wondered if they had found the gelding, and how much time I had left. I think it was now that I became aware that there wasn't much hope for me. All the same, I wasn't going to make it easy for them. I struggled to my feet and gasped with pain as every bone in my bruised body protested. Putting my weight on my leg nearly had me on my knees again, so I reversed the rifle and putting the stock of it under my armpit, used it as a crutch to take one shrieking step after another.

Tortuously, I made my way through the dip of the black valley, limping badly. Once I startled a small animal that rose and darted away into the low undergrowth, making the sweat bead on my forehead, and setting my heart pounding till I shook. I stood then at the base of the next hill and saw its silhouette rise, impossibly high, densely thicketed, and the crown of it lost against the wheeling stars. There was hope there. Perhaps I could lose them in that maze of low bushes, and I crept towards them. The thing I needed most was rest; my head was whirling with exhaustion, and I couldn't even think of what the morning would bring. Somewhere in my guts a pulsing fear smouldered and burst into flame. Sleep was overwhelming me, causing me to stagger as though I were whisky-drunk and the irony of it all quirked my lips upwards even though I was a hell of a long way from laughing.

The bushes clutched at my torn clothes, and I was among them. My legs felt liquid and I suddenly fell, the rifle sliding from my hands. In a panic, I snatched it, seeing its metallic gleam in the darkness and felt a warm rush of relief as my fingers closed around the barrel. Holding it close, I crawled on all fours into the deepest bush, dragging my injured leg behind me, and gratefully, at last, rolled on to my back and lay still.

It was dark in that bush, with even the bright stars blotted from view, and blessedly peaceful. I threw my arm over my eyes, just for a moment, just for a rest, then knew nothing more.

When I awoke, it was with a start, the hair prickling on my neck with a sense of danger, fear drying my mouth. Dawn was in the air, for I could make out individual branches in my lair and a few of the nearest leaves. I was wet with dew and stiff from the running and falling I had done. Raising myself on an elbow, I parted the branches with one cautious hand and peered out, back the way I had come.

The sky was not yet light, though details of the surrounding countryside were more discernible, and high above me, on the slopes of that first hill, spread out like ants, moving slowly, guns in their hands, the posse was searching. Every rock, every niche, every bush came under scrutiny and there must have been twenty of them. They sure were out to get me.

I lay back with a groan. That goddam leg of mine was shot with a piercing pain that was more severe than any I had felt. I didn't want to look at it, but I forced myself to draw up my knee and raise my pants leg. Above my boot, the flesh was swollen to twice its normal size, shiny and red, even in that dim light. I could see it still visibly swelling, fit to burst the leather from my foot and lie there exposed and pulsing with heat and pain. If I had had a knife, I could have tried to cut the boot from my foot. Even so, with fumbling, cold-numbed fingers I unlaced the boot and tried to pull the opening apart to ease the pressure but the wetness of the leather and the push of the flesh inside did little to comfort me. I had to bear with it. It was broken, I guessed.

At last, I raised myself from my torpor and reached for the rifle. The light was growing steadily stronger and the sky was paling. On the hillside, the figures of the hunters had moved steadily down and nearer, they were silent and concentrating, probably as nervous as I was, each one half expecting the sudden crash of a bullet as he uncovered a hiding-place. I took my eyes from them to break open the gun and examine the barrel to see if it had picked up any blockage from being used as a crutch. Thank God for the hard, dry earth, it was dusty but empty. I pushed in a cartridge and closed up the gun. There was no point in running now, even if I could, they'd see any movement for sure. I'd have to sit here and take my chances and hope my bush would be overlooked. It was a big hill, with acres of undergrowth. Even twenty men couldn't pick over every inch. So I waited, watching them come nearer.

They were too clever to move in a single line, abreast. They were dotted around, some ahead, some to the rear. When they reached the valley the leaders were already coming up the slope when the followers were out of sight in the dip. That way, there was always someone covering the others, and at no time was my part of the hill unobserved. I was choking on the feeling of being trapped, and my heart was pounding with the sudden desire to get this thing over and done with. I think if I could have run I would have made a break for it, taking my chances and zig-zagging through the bushes, almost hoping for a quick, merciful bullet, but I could hardly move, lying there like a crippled fox waiting for the hounds to close in.

As they came towards me, I could see the details of their

faces as the light grew. They all seemed to be looking my way, and if they hadn't kept stopping to search someplace I'd have felt sure they could see me. I forced myself to keep still and make my breathing light and shallow, though I don't know what good that did me. None, I guess, Byrnes was well to the fore, his badge shiny on his breast. He must have found the three dead men up there in the rocks, and I didn't fool myself that he would show me any mercy now. He must have hated me more than ever. To one side of him, some distance away and on a level with my hiding-place, another man walked. His hat was pulled down over his eyes, his face black with shadow, but he was familiar somehow. I squinted, trying to make him out, but gave up. The light was too poor, yet.

They moved inexorably up, coming among the bushes, and the nearest were only yards away. I shrank back, curling up and holding my breath, the rifle ready. Maybe I could take one with me when I went. The dark man by Byrnes was below me, his lowered hat visible, standing on a line with my bush, a few feet away. Slowly I levelled the rifle, my finger on the trigger, waiting for him to step up to me. He looked up then, saw my bush and began to walk towards it, pushing his hat back as he did so. At the same time, I saw who he was and that he was unarmed and in that split second my finger tightened involuntarily.

If I could have taken back one action of all my actions in all my life, I would have taken back that one. The man my bullet found was Jed.

He saw me at the same time as the gun exploded. I watched it all in his eyes, shock, horror, fear and, heaven help me, disbelieving brotherly affection. I wasn't even aware of it when the others surrounded me.

CHAPTER FIFTEEN

THEY told me, later, that Jed had refused a gun. He hadn't joined the posse as one of them. There was some remnant of familial feeling, maybe even pity in him that made him think he could get me back, somehow, with no more hurt on either side. He had said, 'Self defence. Man, you can't hang him for protecting himself. Let me try. He'll come back with me, and when it's over and he's served his time, he'll be fine, I know he will.'

So they got me for his murder, and those other three, but those last make no never mind to me. It's Jed I care about and he's the one who has haunted me all these weeks in this cell, waiting for my leg to heal so that I could stand trial, strong and fit and healthy and knowing full well the import of it all. I wrote this while I had nothing to do, while the bone in my ankle knitted slowly, and after all that time the trial was over before you could blink an eye. Wrapped up, tied up, finished.

I wonder if they'll give Ilse these notebooks and what she'll think about it all. I have not seen her, she hasn't visited me, and she did not even come to the courthouse.

Abbie came to see me a couple of times. She's very good hearted, but she cried a lot and that don't help my feelings any so I had to request that she was kept away.

There isn't much time left, so I guess I'll finish it right here. With only a trace of a limp I'll manage those gallows steps easily in the morning. I wouldn't like folks to think I was hesitating in any way. It'll soon be daylight, and I think I'm glad it's over!

NEL BESTSELLERS

Crime

T031 306	THE UNPLEASANTNESS AT THE BELLONA CLUB	*Dorothy L. Sayers*	85p
T031 373	STRONG POISON	*Dorothy L. Sayers*	80p
T032 884	FIVE RED HERRINGS	*Dorothy L. Sayers*	75p

Fiction

T034 879	CRUSADER'S TOMB	*A. J. Cronin*	£1.00
T034 925	HATTER'S CASTLE	*A. J. Cronin*	£1.50
T027 228	THE SPANISH GARDNER	*A. J. Cronin*	45p
T013 936	THE JUDAS TREE	*A. J. Cronin*	50p
T015 386	THE NORTHERN LIGHT	*A. J. Cronin*	50p
T034 755	THE CITADEL	*A. J. Cronin*	£1.10
T027 112	BEYOND THIS PLACE	*A. J. Cronin*	30p
T016 609	KEYS OF THE KINGDOM	*A. J. Cronin*	60p
T029 158	THE STARS LOOK DOWN	*A. J. Cronin*	£1.00
T034 852	THREE LOVES	*A. J. Cronin*	£1.25
T031 594	THE LONELY LADY	*Harold Robbins*	£1.25
T038 114	THE DREAM MERCHANTS	*Harold Robbins*	£1.50
T031 705	THE PIRATE	*Harold Robbins*	£1.00
T033 791	THE CARPETBAGGERS	*Harold Robbins*	£1.25
T035 239	WHERE LOVE HAS GONE	*Harold Robbins*	£1.25
T032 647	THE ADVENTURERS	*Harold Robbins*	£1.25
T038 130	THE INHERITORS	*Harold Robbins*	£1.25
T035 427	STILETTO	*Harold Robbins*	£1.00
T038 092	NEVER LEAVE ME	*Harold Robbins*	£1.00
T032 698	NEVER LOVE A STRANGER	*Harold Robbins*	95p
T032 531	A STONE FOR DANNY FISHER	*Harold Robbins*	90p
T037 053	79 PARK AVENUE	*Harold Robbins*	£1.25
T038 084	THE BETSY	*Harold Robbins*	£1.25
T035 689	RICH MAN, POOR MAN	*Irwin Shaw*	£1.50
T034 720	EVENING IN BYZANTIUM	*Irwin Shaw*	85p
T031 330	THE MAN	*Irving Wallace*	£1.50
T034 283	THE PRIZE	*Irving Wallace*	£1.50
T033 376	THE PLOT	*Irving Wallace*	£1.25
T030 253	THE THREE SIRENS	*Irving Wallace*	£1.25
T033 171	SEVEN MINUTES	*Irving Wallace*	£1.25

Historical

T022 250	THE LADY FOR A RANSOM	*Alfred Duggan*	50p
T017 958	FOUNDING FATHERS	*Alfred Duggan*	50p
T035 050	LEOPARDS AND LILIES	*Alfred Duggan*	90p
T035 131	LORD GEOFFREY'S FANCY	*Alfred Duggan*	75p
T024 903	THE KING OF ATHELNEY	*Alfred Duggan*	60p
T032 817	FOX 1: PRESS GANG	*Adam Hardy*	50p
T032 825	FOX 2: PRIZE MONEY	*Adam Hardy*	50p
T032 833	FOX 3: SIEGE	*Adam Hardy*	50p
T032 841	FOX 4: TREASURE	*Adam Hardy*	50p
T028 092	FOX 14: CLOSE QUARTERS	*Adam Hardy*	50p

Science Fiction

T027 724	SCIENCE FICTION ART	*Brian Aldiss*	£2.95
T030 245	TIME ENOUGH FOR LOVE	*Robert Heinlein*	£1.25
T034 674	STRANGER IN A STRANGE LAND	*Robert Heinlein*	£1.20
T037 045	I WILL FEAR NO EVIL	*Robert Heinlein*	£1.20
T030 467	STARMAN JONES	*Robert Heinlein*	75p
T026 817	THE HEAVEN MAKERS	*Frank Herbert*	35p
T035 697	DUNE	*Frank Herbert*	£1.25